Appointment
with a
Stranger

Jean Thesman

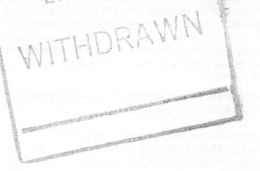

M

MACMILLAN CHILDREN'S BOOKS

First published in the United States of America 1989 by
Houghton Mifflin Company, Boston

First published in the United Kingdom 1990 by
MACMILLAN CHILDREN'S BOOKS
A division of Macmillan Publishers Limited
London and Basingstoke
Associated companies throughout the world

ISBN 0-333-53219-8

A CIP catalogue record for this book is available from the British Library

Printed by the Western Book Company Ltd, Bristol

This is for the storytellers who gathered for tea on Thursdays a long time ago: Mama, Mary, Arliss, and the Helens.

Now it's my turn.

Appointment with a Stranger

One

"So where were you yesterday?"

The tall, brown-haired boy sitting in front of me had turned around, and when I didn't answer him, he knocked his fist on my desk. "Hello? Hello? Drew Sennett calling Madame X. Come in, please."

In spite of myself, I grinned. "Don't talk so loud," I told him. "You should be copying what the teacher wrote on the board."

"Miss Packer doesn't care if we don't copy that stuff," he said without lowering his voice.

"How do you know?"

"I had her for sophomore English last year." He didn't notice when Miss Packer stopped writing and turned around to stare at the back of his head.

Embarrassed, I slouched in my seat. Miss Packer smiled faintly at me.

I

"Drew is our class comedian," she said. She nodded her approval when Drew whipped around and sat up straight. "But I recommend that after this you regard his suggestions as stumbling blocks on the way to a high school diploma."

Everyone in class laughed, including Drew. When Miss Packer turned back to the board, I pulled a pencil out of my book bag and began writing. I wasn't sure what I'd missed the day before, the second day of school, but I was resigned to the problems that went with frequent absences and the extra effort I always had to make. And certainly, I didn't want to ask anybody if there'd been a homework assignment yesterday. Someone might join Drew in getting curious about where I'd been.

When the bell rang for the end of first period I stood up quickly, intending to hurry out, but Drew was at my elbow, poking up his glasses and obviously intending to walk out to the hall with me.

"So tell me your name again," he said. "I don't think I heard you right the first day."

"I didn't tell you," I answered quietly. I slung my bag over my right shoulder since he walked on my right side, forcing him to move over.

He laughed, showing braces on his teeth. "What's the secret, new girl? Everybody will know your name before the first week is over, so you might as well tell me now. Let me guess. Your mother named you after your astrological sign and your rich old aunt's favorite breakfast cereal. You're Saggitarius Alpo, right?"

He was ridiculous, but I had to laugh. "Alpo is dog food."

"It's what my little brother eats for breakfast," Drew told me. He poked at his glasses once more and peered at me. "Come on, what's your name?"

"Keller Parrish," I said, giving up. I dug my class schedule out of my pocket and showed him. "See? I didn't make it up."

He studied my schedule. "I didn't think you did. Hmm. We've got the same lunch. How come I didn't see you yesterday?"

Questions. "I don't always eat lunch," I told him and I stopped walking. "Here's my next class. I'll see you."

"Like during lunch," he said. "You have to eat and you have to sit somewhere so you might as well sit at my table."

"Maybe," I said vaguely, turning away from him. He was like a big, loose-jointed puppy, cute and friendly, but too curious.

For a moment I couldn't remember where I'd sat in this room on Tuesday. It was an art class and we used drawing boards. Already half the places were taken. Hadn't I been in the back, my favorite spot? I made my way there, hoping I was right. I'd felt so awful Tuesday, the first day of school, that I hadn't paid much attention to anything. Tentatively, I dropped my book bag beside the last drawing board, and the girl next to it smiled at me.

"Where were you yesterday?" she asked.

"Home," I murmured without looking at her. I found my portfolio on the shelf below the tilted board, and I took out the drawing I'd been working on. It was embarrassingly bad.

3

"That's very nice," the girl said generously, bending over my board. "I was watching you Tuesday. I could tell you weren't feeling well."

"I'm fine now," I said. But the tightness was building up in my chest again. Relax, I told myself. Do what Dr. Mercer taught you. Let your shoulders drop and think, You're safe, Keller. Everything's going to be all right.

I remembered that the girl's name was Rose Mackey. She didn't speak to me again. At first I felt relieved, but then, glancing over at her, I was sorry. To make up for my rudeness, I stopped by her board when class was over and looked at her drawing before she put it away. Rose had drawn the trees outside the windows. She was a wonderful artist and I told her so.

Her round face lit up. "Thanks, Keller. I really appreciate that. Listen, we've got the same trig class, so let's walk together."

I couldn't refuse without being rude all over again. Maybe she even had the same lunch that I had and I could sit with her instead of curious, noisy Drew. Rose seemed like a safer friend. Or rather, a safer acquaintance. People who are sick all the time only disappoint themselves if they try to have friends.

Rose and I were opposites. I was thin, with straight red hair, while she was tall and a little overweight, with thick, curly dark hair, and skin that glowed. She smiled at everyone. I felt self-conscious walking beside her.

We hurried to class. The tightness was back in my chest, and I was trying to force air out of my lungs without wheezing, but Rose heard me anyway and stopped. "You have asthma, don't you?" she said. "So

4

does my mother. Do you want me to go down to the nurse's office with you?''

I shook my head hastily. "No, thanks. I went on Tuesday and believe me, she doesn't help.''

Rose laughed. "She's an awful old cow, isn't she? Don't ever go there for cramps. The first thing she asks is if you're pregnant. I guess she hasn't heard that you're not likely to have a period if you're pregnant.'' Rose had a great laugh.

In trig, she pointed out my seat to me — I'd forgotten that one, too — and whispered, "We'll have lunch together. Okay?''

I nodded and pulled my book out of my bag. On the bottom of the bag my little pillbox rattled, reminding me that I was supposed to turn it over to the nurse for safekeeping. But I wouldn't. Leaving it in someone else's hands — especially someone as cold and uninterested as the school nurse — didn't sound very safe to me. I'd learned by some scary experiences that it wasn't smart to trust my problems to indifferent strangers at school.

At lunch, Rose and I sat alone on one side of the cafeteria. I could see crazy Drew Sennett making everyone laugh at a table in the center, and when Rose saw me watching, she said, "I usually sit there, but I didn't think you were up to Drew yet.''

"I'm fine,'' I said, not wanting to join Drew but wanting Rose to understand that I wasn't an invalid and a complete drag. Not yet, anyway.

"I meant that you're probably not up to Drew, since you're new in school,'' Rose said. "He takes getting used to, like broccoli or control-top pantyhose.''

My soup spoon wobbled on the way to my mouth. "I laugh at practically anything, so if you're going to say something else like that, wait until I'm finished with my soup," I told her.

"You bet," she said cheerfully. "But you're in worse trouble already, because here comes Drew."

I looked up. Drew loped across the room, grinning. "I've been waiting for you, Scorpio grape-nuts," he said as he plopped down next to me. "How come you're sitting with the woman I love?"

I glanced at Rose and saw that she was laughing, so I laughed, too. "We're having a private conversation," I told him.

"There are no secrets in this school," Drew said. He helped himself to crackers from my tray and Rose slapped his hand. He shrugged, dug in his pocket, and gave me a chocolate bar. "Take this in trade for the crackers."

I pushed it away. I couldn't eat chocolate. "No thanks."

"What a grouch," he complained, but he got to his feet. "Maybe tomorrow both of you ladies will sit with me so we can discuss the meaning of life and why the cafeteria food is being poisoned by the teachers."

"Get out of here, Drew," Rose said. "Can't you see that Keller isn't impressed?"

Drew slapped his palm against his chest. "You're breaking my heart, Mackey. I'm mad for you and you're throwing me out."

"Good-bye!" Rose shouted, laughing. After he left, she said, "I think he's got a crush on you already."

6

"I thought he loved you."

"Of course not," she scoffed. "We grew up climbing fences and stealing apples together."

I pushed my empty bowl away. Climbing fences and stealing apples. "It must be nice, living in the country," I responded politely to her somewhat alarming statement.

"You'll find out," Rose said. "Now that you live in Cascade, too."

On my way home that afternoon, I thought about what she'd said. The school bus rumbled over endless rough and narrow roads, letting kids off at long driveways or sometimes by the gates to fenced fields. I was homesick for Seattle's sidewalks and parks. The country, like Drew Sennett, broccoli, and control-top pantyhose, would also take some getting used to.

Grandmother was home, waiting for me in the kitchen with a glass of fresh orange juice. "Your mother called to see how you are today. She was glad that you made it to school."

"I nearly always do," I told her. "No big deal."

I could see that Grandmother was trying as hard to be casual as I was. Quickly, before she started worrying out loud again, I said, "Did Mom say anything else?"

"She's not sure they can come for another visit very soon."

"That's okay," I said. I was disappointed, though. And fully aware of how much trouble I was causing my family. If it hadn't been for me, they wouldn't be moving away from the city.

7

"You'll be an old-timer in Cascade by the time they move," she said as she shoved a plate of oatmeal cookies toward me. "You can show 'em the ropes."

"Sure."

"You feeling all right?"

"I'm great, honestly. Sorry about yesterday."

She pushed her curly white hair away from her forehead and blinked unhappily. "You frightened me. I never realized how far away that hospital in North Grange is until I had to drive there with somebody who was choking."

"I wasn't choking," I said. "I'm sorry you were scared."

"You're braver than I am." Grandmother nudged the plate. "Aren't you going to eat these cookies?"

"I'll save them until after my walk," I told her. I got away from her, hurrying upstairs to my bedroom, trying not to listen to her worrying and fretting behind me. It made me feel guilty.

"I'll never understand your doctor," I heard her say from the stairs. "You should be resting, especially after yesterday."

I changed into jeans and a loose cotton shirt, and ran back downstairs.

Grandmother was waiting. "Please be careful. I'll be looking for you in an hour. Don't tire yourself."

Impulsively, I kissed her. "I'll be fine," I promised, and I took off.

My doctor had prescribed one hour of walking every day after school in the clean country air. I hurried down the road until I no longer felt Grandmother's eyes on

8

me. She was trying hard to take good care of me and I knew I made her anxious. I was relieved when the house was out of sight.

The road led between open fields, around a long curve at the base of a wooded hill, to an old farm. "That's Deerfield Pond," Grandmother had said when I asked about the place after I first arrived in Cascade. "It's beautiful, but there's no one living there now."

I left the dusty road and walked through a field toward the willows that surrounded the pond. My shirt stuck to my back. The sun seemed hotter here. The afternoon was so still that I could hear insects in the grass at my feet.

I went closer to the pond than I had before. A log was half buried in the grass, and I sat down on it, pulled off my sneakers, and thrust my feet in the water. It was as warm as bath water and dusted with late summer pollen.

I hadn't been swimming for years. Chlorinated pools made me sick. Public beaches carried the dangers of infection and floating dust and pollen. What promised to be fun for everyone else guaranteed a panicked struggle to breathe for me. I was behaving irresponsibly by even kicking my feet in the pond water.

But, oh, it was marvelous! It looked shallow, not dangerous. And perhaps the pollen glimmering on the surface was not the kind that made me ill. I might be able to swim here safely.

Don't be silly, I thought. I wasn't wearing a swimsuit.

But there's no one here to see, I told myself.

I stripped off my jeans, hurrying so I wouldn't have a chance to be sensible, and waded into the water. It was deeper than I'd thought. When it was deep enough, I slid down until only my head was above the surface. This is perfect, I thought. Heaven. I stretched out on my back, keeping afloat by gently moving my arms. Over me the September sky was bright and empty.

Did I still know how to swim? I turned over on my stomach, kicked hard, and stretched out my arms. Suddenly I was struggling for breath.

Stand up! I tried to get my feet under me, but the water was over my head. Desperately I turned toward shore. The pond, moments before so innocent and safe, pulled me down, strangled me, terrified me. I'd have screamed, if I could have drawn a breath.

"Stop struggling!" someone shouted. I felt an arm circle me from behind and I turned and grabbed it.

"No!" the stranger shouted. "Let go. I'll keep you up."

But I was so frightened I couldn't let go of him. To my horror, he pushed me away, hard.

"Relax! I'll take care of you!"

He ducked, then came up behind me and tugged me toward shore. As soon as I could touch bottom, I stood up, but he didn't let go of me. I still couldn't get my breath.

"You're safe now," he said. "Relax." When I couldn't answer, he picked me up bodily and carried me out of the water.

A large brown dog danced excitedly on the grass. When

the boy put me down, the dog jumped on me. The boy spoke sharply to him.

I tried to walk toward my clothes, but my knees buckled and I fell. The boy knelt beside me and helped me sit up.

"Don't panic," he said. "Here. Let me rub your back. You'll be all right in a minute."

I flinched under his strong fingers, but I wasn't able to pull away. He found sore places deep in the muscles in my back and rubbed them hard, until at last I could exhale all the air trapped in my lungs.

I put my hands over my face and bent my head, fully aware of how I must look.

"I'll get your clothes," he said, reading my mind.

I didn't look up, not even when he dropped my jeans and sneakers in front of me.

"Don't feel bad," he said. "I look pretty strange myself."

I glanced up at him then, grateful for his tact. His dark curly hair was plastered to his face, and his eyes were the same color as the pond, a curious green glimmering with gold.

"I'm Tom Hurley," he said. "I live here. Who are you?"

When he smiled, he was beautiful.

Two

I told him my name reluctantly. I was pulling my fingers through my hair, trying to comb it, assuring myself that it didn't matter how I looked. He'd saved me from drowning, and that's all he could be thinking about.

"Thanks for helping me," I said. "I'm not a very good swimmer."

"When I first saw you, you were doing pretty well." He pushed his hair back and wiped water off his face with a lean, tanned hand. "I wasn't expecting to see anybody out there, so you surprised me. For a minute I forgot all about the beaver traps, and when you went under, I was afraid that you'd been caught."

I stared at him. "There are traps under the water?"

The dog leaned against him and Tom patted him. "Troy here got caught in one, and I think there are more."

"Who would trap beavers here? That's so mean." I was ready to cry, just thinking about it.

"There's a guy who lives on the other side of town — Elwood Bruce. He set the traps for the beavers and told me about it at school. The jerk." Tom pulled Troy down beside him and hugged him suddenly. "I left school as soon as he told me and ran all the way home. When I didn't see Troy, I knew what must have happened. Troy's always chasing after the beavers, even though he can't catch them. And then I saw him under the water. I was sure he was dead."

"Troy's lucky you left school when you did," I said, shivering, but not because I was cold. I looked out across the pond and almost expected to see a beaver struggling for its life.

"I'd hate to lose my dog," Tom said.

"Where's the beaver dam?" I asked. I didn't know much about beavers except that they built dams across creeks to make ponds for themselves.

Tom gestured toward the other side of the pond. "It's over there. It looks different somehow." He seemed puzzled by something.

But then he looked at me suddenly and grinned. "Do you want to come over to the house? My mother's there. After you call your family and tell them you're all right, we'll have some lemonade."

I wouldn't dare call Grandmother! I stood up suddenly. "Thanks, but I have to get going. My grandmother will be worried about me and I'm afraid a telephone call won't help."

"Who's your grandmother?" Tom asked. "I know most of the people around here."

"Beth Parrish. Mrs. Paul Parrish," I said, "but my grandfather died after they moved here a couple of years ago."

Tom shook his head. "Gee, I don't remember anyone named Parrish."

"She lives about two miles down the road," I said. "I'm staying with her for a while." I smiled at him. "Thanks again. I won't forget what you did for me."

He shrugged, his shoulders strong and square under his wet white shirt. I could see that I was embarrassing him. "It wasn't hard," he said.

He walked with me across the field, but Troy lingered behind us. When I looked back, I saw that the dog was holding up one paw.

"I think your dog is hurt," I said.

He looked back and stopped. "That's the foot he caught in the trap," he said. "Can you wait a minute? I'd better get Troy in the house and see if I can help him."

"It was just today that he got caught?" I asked. I'd somehow gotten the idea that the adventure with the trap had been a long time before.

"It happened this morning. Will you wait?"

"I can't, honestly. It's all right. Take Troy inside."

He ran back toward the dog and waved to me. "I'll see you again," he called. "Take care of yourself."

I watched while he picked up the dog and carried him toward an old house I could barely see through the trees south of the pond. For a moment I was tempted to run after him, telephone Grandmother, and then help him take care of the dog. But Grandmother would want to know everything, and if I told her that Tom had rescued me from drowning in the pond, she'd panic and I'd feel guiltier than ever.

I'd really scared her the day before when my pills and inhaler didn't work, and she'd had to take me to the emergency room for treatment. When we got home, she'd phoned Mom and Dad, and for a while I thought she was going to ask them to come and get me because she was convinced that she didn't know how to take care of me. She wouldn't believe that it wasn't her fault. My parents must have worked hard to reassure her because I was still in Cascade.

I didn't want to cause her any more worry, so I hurried toward the road. When I looked back, Tom was no longer in sight. My shirt was nearly dry, so my appearance wouldn't give me away. The sun seemed even hotter now, the air smelled wonderful, and I broke into an easy little jog.

I, Keller Parrish, was jogging.

I stopped and stared at my feet as if they could explain this. I hadn't run anywhere since I was seven years old and first got sick.

Suddenly, exultantly, I threw my arms up in the air and jumped as high as I could. Then, before the mood wore off, I started running again, and ran until I was breathless. But this wasn't the kind of breathlessness that terrified me. This was a healthy kind, where I could exhale freely. I didn't feel as if old, used-up air was trapped in my lungs, leaving no room for good air. I felt — normal.

I'd almost drowned that afternoon, and instead of having a terrible reaction, I was actually feeling wonderful. I wasn't sure what had happened to me, but I wasn't going to spoil it by prompting Grandmother to ask questions, so I stopped running before I came in sight of Grandmother's house.

She was in her garden picking squash when I came up the driveway. I hurried up to my room and was changing clothes quickly when I heard the kitchen screen door slam.

"Keller, are you all right?" Grandmother called.

"Yes," I shouted down from my bedroom door.

"Did you have a nice walk? You didn't tire yourself out, did you?" I could almost feel the tension in her voice. She was wondering if she was going to have to drive me to the hospital again.

"No, but I'm really hungry." There. That would reassure her. "Do you suppose I could have a sandwich before dinner?"

Grandmother laughed. "Come down to the kitchen. I'll give you anything you want."

I studied myself in the mirror while I brushed my hair. My face had just a hint of sunburn. For the first time I could remember, I was pretty. And I hoped that I'd looked that way to Tom.

I ate two sandwiches and drank a glass of water while Grandmother prepared the squash for baking. I was curious about Tom and couldn't resist asking her a guarded question.

"I thought I saw a boy going into that house by Deerfield Pond," I said. "Do you suppose someone lives there after all?"

"I'm sure it's empty," she said. She looked at me suddenly. "It might have been a vagrant, someone dangerous. Maybe you shouldn't walk that far down the road anymore."

I gathered up my plate and glass and took them to the sink. "No, I think there's a woman at the house, too. A boy and his mother, I bet."

"Hmm." Grandmother sliced the squash with a sharp knife. "Well, it would be nice to have neighbors there. I don't always like living in the last house on the road. It gets lonely." She looked up at me again, smiling. "Well, it used to be lonely. With you here, and your parents coming to live in Cascade before winter, I guess I'm not going to mind whether this is the last occupied house on the road or not."

"I think it's not," I told her confidently.

I woke up twice that night, which wasn't unusual. Most nights I had to use my inhaler. But the first time I woke, it was because of a disturbing dream and not because I was having trouble breathing again.

I dreamed that I was standing by a window watching rain falling, and Tom came. He stood outside under the window, looking up at me, urgently telling me something. But I couldn't hear him. I tried to shove the window open but it stuck, and Tom was moving away from me so that I could hardly see him any longer. When I got the window open at last, he was gone. I leaned out into the rain and called his name over and over, but he

17

never answered me. It seemed to me, though, that I could hear his dog, Troy, barking a long way away.

The second time I woke that night, I was struggling to breathe again. After the medicated mist in the inhaler started to work, I got out of bed and went to the window. A clear yellow moon floated high in the sky, and I looked down, half expecting to see Tom and his dog looking up at me. I couldn't understand why I felt so sad.

I'll see him again, I told myself as I crawled back in bed. Tom Hurley had saved my life, so of course we'd meet again.

Three

The next morning, Friday, rain began falling during my art class. I watched it from my drawing board, wondering how long it would last and if I'd dare try getting past Grandmother to go for a walk that afternoon. I liked walking in the rain, but I doubted if she'd think it was a suitable form of recreation for someone like me. But if I didn't walk out toward Deerfield Pond, I might not see Tom that day, because I hadn't been able to find him at school.

I bent over my drawing and carefully erased a line. Rose will know him, I thought. She's lived in Cascade all her life. There isn't another high school in town so he must be a student here.

Of course, I wasn't really expecting something like friendship to develop between Tom and me. And I wouldn't expect anything more complicated, either, not when I didn't know how long it would be before I made an idiot out of myself by getting sick at the wrong time. I tried hard never to indulge myself in romantic fantasies. But, oh, it wasn't always easy.

At lunch, while Rose and I stood in the cafeteria line, I asked her if she knew Tom Hurley.

"Tom who?" She was struggling to decide between a dried-up brownie and a small square of carrot cake.

"Hurley. He lives past me on Birch Road, in the old house by the pond." I took a piece of the carrot cake.

"That place has been empty for as long as I can remember," she said. She took a brownie and a piece of carrot cake.

"I talked to him yesterday," I said. "He even invited me in the house, but I had to hurry home."

"For heaven's sake," Rose said, surprised. "I'll have to tell Mama about that. She picks blackberries near the pond and she'd better not go again if someone's living there."

I followed her to the center table, where Drew already sat with some of his friends. I was tempted to hang back, maybe tell Rose that I had some reading I had to do and needed to be alone, but she didn't give me a chance.

"Here's the new girl," she said. "She's been in Cascade High long enough now to be able to stand the shock of meeting you guys."

"She knows me already," Drew said. He put his hand over his heart with an exaggerated flourish. "Everybody, meet the girl I've been waiting for all my life — Miss Capricorn Froot Loops."

"Keller Parrish," I said, correcting him and having a hard time looking cranky. He was ridiculous. And sweet in a weird way. I sat down next to him, not because I really wanted to, but because everyone seemed to expect it.

"Keller's a wonderful name," a small, dark girl said. "I'm Jane Hammond."

She told me that the boy sitting next to her was Max Hendricks. He smiled at me, but he looked back at Jane right away. "You want my dessert, Jane?" he asked.

"They're in love," Drew told me, without bothering to lower his voice. "But we let them sit here anyway."

Someone else joined us, Sig Munson, a tall, blue-eyed boy with lashes as pale as his hair. He blushed when he saw me and then looked away, so neither one of us had to say hello. "Drew, the junior counselor's looking for you again," he said, poking Drew's shoulder. "What did you do this time?"

Everyone laughed. Drew drank the last of the milk in his carton and threw his arm around me. "Will you meet me after school? We'll run away together before I'm caught and locked up."

I slipped free of his arm. "I have to go straight home."

"Good. I have to go straight to your house, too, so I'll give you a ride." He got up and trotted off, waving at kids, even waving at the kitchen staff. They laughed at him, too.

"He's crazy," I said to Rose.

"Sure," she responded cheerfully. "Everybody likes him anyway. Why don't you ask him about that boy you met yesterday? Drew knows everyone."

I nodded but I wasn't sure I wanted to do that. I was almost certain that Drew liked me a little more than he should, and so it would be tacky to ask him about another boy. But then, I thought, reconsidering, that would certainly turn Drew off before he even had a chance to find out about me. Not even Drew, with his wacky sense of humor, would be able to cope with a girl who sometimes couldn't breathe, who actually wheezed when she danced.

The carrot cake was awful but I ate it. If my mouth was busy chewing, I wouldn't be tempted to talk. If I didn't talk, I wasn't likely to make too many friends. And if I didn't have too many friends, there wouldn't be many opportunities for people to hurt my feelings. No one could say that I didn't learn from experience.

But before I left the cafeteria, I looked around carefully, hoping that I'd see Tom somewhere. He wasn't there, and I didn't see him anyplace else that day, either.

Drew was waiting by my locker after school. "I'm here, ready to deliver you to your grandmother," he said.

"How did you know where my locker is and how did you find out that I live with my grandmother?" I asked, fascinated in spite of myself.

"I applied subtle forms of torture to Rose," he said. "She confessed everything."

I pulled my jacket out of the locker. "I really ought to take the bus," I said. "I don't think Grandmother is prepared for company this afternoon." Somehow I'd have to turn off his enthusiasm.

"Grandmothers love me," he protested. "Parents love me. Who would think that a guy with an innocent face like mine was actually a raving sex maniac?"

"My grandmother reads minds."

"Oh, lord, I'm sunk then." He took my book bag away from me and grabbed my hand. "Come on, Keller, let's get going. Maybe your granny will fix us a sandwich before she throws me out."

"She'll throw you out if you call her Granny," I told him.

"Will she let me kiss you first?" he asked suddenly.

I pushed him away. "Quit that. It's not funny."

"Just testing," he said jovially. "My car's in the back lot. Duck your head and let's run."

He darted off through the rain, but I didn't run after him. There was the warning tightness in my chest. I remembered suddenly that I'd forgotten to take my pill at lunch. I followed Drew slowly, trying to take long, slow breaths, relaxing my shoulders. I couldn't be sick going home in the car, I just couldn't. What I needed most was a few seconds of privacy to take my inhaler out of my pocket and use it. But I was surrounded by kids, and there was no way I was going to humiliate myself in front of them. I walked on, trying not to panic.

"Jeez," Drew said when I finally reached his car, "you must be half duck."

"Three-quarters duck and one-quarter water witch," I said as I got in beside him.

"I think I like that water witch part," he said. "Onward, to scare the Highland fling out of Granny."

"Don't call her Granny," I said, alarmed. "Call her Mrs. Parrish. She's not the granny type."

Drew's car started with a roar. "My granny's not the granny type either. Actually, we have to go pull her out of Bernie's Truckstop and Video Palace every Friday night before they call the sheriff.''

I started laughing. "I don't believe you. What an awful thing to say about your grandmother.''

"My granny *is* awful," Drew said. "We're all scared of her.''

His nonsense cheered me up, and I almost forgot that I was close to embarrassing myself with an audible struggle to exhale.

"Rose told me you had asthma," he said, catching me off guard. "Go ahead and wheeze. Granny does it all the time. When she gets too bad, we put her out on the porch so we don't have to listen.''

I shouted with laughter and began breathing a lot better. I relaxed against the back of the seat. The windshield wipers batted at the rain and the car radio was turned to a station that played my favorite kind of quiet music. Nice.

"Straight out Birch Road past Five Corners, last house on the left," Drew said. "Did Rose tell it right?''

"Yes," I said. Here was my chance. "Do you know the people who live at the end of Birch Road?''

"Nobody lives in that house," Drew said. "But there are some big goldfish in the pond. I ought to know because they're my goldfish. I turned them loose a long time ago and they started growing. They even had babies. Sometimes I go out there and feed them dried ant eggs for a special treat.''

"I'm sure I saw people around there," I said, but Drew only shrugged.

When we pulled in the driveway, I saw Grandmother

watching us from the living room window She had the front door open by the time we reached the porch.

"Drew Sennett! I'm glad to see you." Grandmother shut the door behind us and reached for our wet jackets. "The rain's getting worse. It was good of you to bring Keller home."

"I really had an important errand to run," Drew said as he made his way familiarly to the kitchen ahead of Grandmother. "But Keller threw a tantrum in the main hall, so I agreed to sacrifice my own plans and give her a ride."

"Hey!" I protested. "That's not how it was."

"I'm used to Drew's nonsense," Grandmother said, laughing. "We're old pals."

Drew sat down at the kitchen table. "I'll have mustard on my bologna sandwich," he said, "and a glass of milk. And by the way, Granny said to tell you that the book you wanted is in, so if you want to check it out before her martial arts class hears about it, you'd better get to the library in the next day or two."

"I thought your own personal grandmother hung around a truck stop," I said as I sat down at the table across from him.

"Keller!" Grandmother said, surprised.

"No, you've got it all wrong," Drew told me. "She hangs around the Blue Chip Topless Bar and Body Shop with a bunch of born-again bikers." He pretended to glare at Grandmother. "Mrs. P., why didn't you offer to fix me up with your red-haired granddaughter when she first moved to town?"

"I didn't want to expose her to Cascade's dark side,"

25

Grandmother said. She was making him a sandwich with two pieces of bologna and a thick slice of cheese.

"Believe it or not, Drew teaches a Sunday school class at church," Grandmother told me. "You should come with me some Sunday."

"We won't let her in," Drew said, reaching for the plate Grandmother handed him. "Does this have plenty of mustard on it or am I going to have to get the jar out myself?"

"It's the way you like it," Grandmother said. She gave me a sandwich without mustard, which was another no-no for me.

"I've got big plans for tonight, Mrs. P.," Drew said, eyes on his sandwich. "A bunch of us are going over to North Grange to see that new movie. You know, the one with all the sex scenes in it that you and Granny liked so much. How about letting Keller go with us?"

"That's a movie about a lost dog," Grandmother countered. "The other movie left Wednesday."

"Trust you to keep up on stuff like that," Drew said.

"I don't think I can go," I said. "I've got a lot of homework. Anyway, I don't really know your friends."

"All the more reason you should go," Grandmother said. "You need to make friends here."

Drew was watching me closely. "We're only going to a movie. You don't have to make a lifetime commitment for that, Keller."

I looked beseechingly at Grandmother.

"Go ahead," Grandmother said. "Just don't stay out late. I'll expect you home by eleven."

Drew looked up, pretending to be horrified. "What

Eleven? I'd planned on bringing her back about noon tomorrow.''

Grandmother shook her head. "Someday someone will take you seriously, Drew, and you'll be in trouble.''

"I was in trouble all day today,'' Drew said as he stood up. "I gotta go, ladies. Keller, I'll pick you up at seven. You don't need any money this time. I'll pay. Next time it's your turn.''

And he was gone, banging the front door behind him.

"He's certainly different,'' I said.

"He's a lot smarter than he pretends,'' Grandmother said. "And he'd make a loyal friend.''

I thought about that when I went upstairs. I wasn't sure exactly what a loyal friend was. One who wouldn't tease you when you were embarrassingly sick, I supposed. One who wouldn't sigh if you had to go home early. One who'd be patient if you fell behind. I wouldn't count on finding one.

Drew picked me up first that night. It was still raining so he came to the door with an umbrella. Sig was already at Rose's house and we picked them up next, then Jane and Max, who were waiting for us at an ice cream store downtown in Cascade.

North Grange was five miles away, down a long, steep highway, and we got there just a few minutes before the movie started. I had a wonderful time, and kept reminding myself that I must not get too attached to the feeling.

Afterward, I was the first one Drew took home. "I have to stay on the good side of your grandmother,'' he said as we walked up the porch steps. "If I'd taken you

27

out for something to eat, we wouldn't have been here by eleven. Bad news. Mrs. P. can be pretty scary."

"You're really crazy," I told him.

He bent and kissed my forehead. "Crazy about you, Taurus Honey Smacks."

Then he ran down the steps and climbed in his car. "Good night, my love," he shouted. "I'll be back at midnight and we'll run away together. I can't marry you because my wife and all my creditors wouldn't like it, but I can promise you a great weekend."

The door opened behind me. Grandmother was laughing. "It's a good thing I don't have any close neighbors," she said.

Well, you do have neighbors, I thought, but not close ones. Tom, where were you tonight? Did you have a date, too?

When will I see you again?

Four

I woke up to sunlight, watery and pale. When I opened my window, the Saturday morning was so quiet that all I could hear was the distant scolding of a crow. It was past eight o'clock, and I was anxious to eat breakfast and walk.

Downstairs, Grandmother stood at the kitchen window drinking coffee. "Good morning, Keller. Have you noticed that the maple leaves are starting to change color?"

"Fall's almost here." I drank half my glass of orange juice while I looked out the window.

"I'm glad you went out with Drew and his friends last night," she said, turning to face me. "Your mother told me that you had a tendency to keep to yourself."

I'd heard the speech Grandmother was about to make a thousand times. I wondered if they, the adults who thought they knew so much about me, had any idea what it was like to be sick the way I was sick. I wasn't a tragic figure wasting away in a hospital with some romantic disease. I had an ugly illness, one that the kids had teased me about in grade school. They quit teasing in high school. Instead, they snickered behind their hands. Did anyone honestly think I didn't hear the nicknames? Wheezy? The Great Gasper? I didn't want close friends, even if anyone wanted to be my close friend, because eventually I'd be the source of embarrassment for them as well as myself. You'd think adults could figure that out.

"I'll probably make lots of friends here, Grandmother," I said to put an end to the lecture before it even began. I sat down and began to eat.

"Do you have plans for today?" Grandmother asked after a while.

"I'm going to take my walk right after breakfast," I told her, avoiding her eyes. Will you be at the pond today, Tom? I wondered.

"I can't understand your doctors," Grandmother complained as she poured more coffee for herself. "I'm sure all that walking can't be good for you. I knew a girl in college who had asthma and she spent most of her free time resting."

"Walking fast strengthens my lungs," I told her. "I really do feel better if I walk every day."

I'd finished my breakfast, so I excused myself. I was anxious to get away before she decided that I ought to see her college friend's doctor and get different advice that would at least make *her* feel better. Poor Grandmother. I'd been through all that with my parents.

I liked walking. I liked being by myself and watching things change as the seasons changed. Cascade was different from Seattle, but I was getting used to it. I was eager to get out into the still, calm morning.

Grandmother let me go, but reluctantly, and I headed toward the end of Birch Road and the pond. About half a mile before I reached it, I stopped and used my inhaler, just in case. The medication made my heart beat faster. I took deep breaths and hurried along, smiling.

There he was. Tom was standing on the opposite side of the pond, almost out of sight under the willows whose leaves drooped over the water. I crossed the field as fast as I could without looking desperate. "Hi, Tom!" I called out. "Tom!"

He'd been looking down into the water, and when I called his name, his head jerked up. For a moment, he seemed stunned, but then he waved and walked toward me. When he got close enough, I saw that he was smiling. So was I.

Troy, his dog, limped behind him. "How's your dog?" I asked.

Tom reached down and touched the dog's head. "His foot still seems sore."

I was close enough to touch the dog, so I stroked his silky brown head. My hand was trembling and I hoped Tom didn't notice. You'd have thought that I'd never talked to a boy before.

"Are you feeling all right?" Tom asked. "I thought about you and wondered how you were getting along. I should have walked home with you."

"I'm fine," I said, remembering that I'd actually jogged on the way home. "Maybe all I needed was a swim in a warm pond."

"I don't think so," Tom said. He didn't realize that I was joking. "You shouldn't swim here."

"I remember," I said. "The beaver traps."

"Trapping is rotten," he said suddenly, angrily. He touched his dog again, as if to reassure both of them. "Sometimes I find traps in the woods around here, too. I break them up."

I nodded. "Good for you. I'll do that, too, if I find any."

Overhead, half a dozen ducks flapped in an uncertain circle over the pond. "They want to land on the water, but they're afraid of Troy," Tom said. "He won't hurt them, but maybe we'd better move off a little way. Would you like to walk in the woods?"

"I'd love it." My heart was beating hard again, but not from the medication.

We walked side by side toward the woods, and when we were far enough away, the ducks splashed down in the pond. Troy didn't look back. He limped patiently at Tom's left side.

We followed a faint, soft path under the trees. "Do you walk here a lot?" I asked Tom.

"Sure," he said. "Troy and the deer and I."

"There are deer here?" I'd never seen a deer up close except in the zoo.

"A few. When we moved here a long time ago, Dad fenced the whole place and put up No Hunting signs all over. Usually the hunters stay out, and the deer learned after a while that they could jump the fence and be safe here with us.''

I ducked under a low-hanging branch. ''You really love animals, don't you?''

He looked down at me, amazed. ''Sure. Don't you?''

I nodded. The zoo in Seattle was one of my favorite places. My folks wouldn't let me have a dog or a cat because I might be allergic to them, even though my friends' pets didn't bother me. But I'd always wanted a pet, any kind. Tom's life here seemed like some sort of magic existence.

''Are there other animals here besides deer?'' I asked.

''Raccoons,'' Tom said. ''Squirrels and chipmunks, of course. A few rabbits. And my dad says there used to be a black bear around here, but I never saw it.''

We crossed a wide creek, jumping from one mossy stone to another. Troy waded in the water and wouldn't come out until Tom called him.

''We're coming to a place where you can look out over the valley,'' Tom said. ''You'll like it.''

He was right. We sat on a long, flat rock and leaned back against a boulder that was taller than Tom. At our feet, the cliff dropped away and we saw miles and miles of forest. Maples and alders, just starting to turn gold, glowed among the firs. Late-blooming dogwoods held up their white stars from the shadows.

''What's on the other side of the forest?'' I asked. A pearly haze hung in the distance.

''North Grange. It's pretty small. There's not much there.''

He surprised me. North Grange was three times the

size of Cascade. But then, Cascade was his home, so he'd naturally think it was the center of everything.

"Do you like Seattle?" I asked. "I've lived there all my life, until now, that is."

He shook his head and laughed gently. "My mom likes it. We go there for concerts sometimes. But Dad and I just aren't city people."

I looked at my watch. "I have to go back," I said reluctantly, and I got to my feet. I hated to leave this place, but I didn't want to worry Grandmother — or tell her about Tom.

Tom stood quickly. "Already? Can't you stay longer?"

"My grandmother will be expecting me," I told him.

We walked back the way we'd come without talking. Troy followed, and his foot seemed better. Once he even ran off the trail in silent pursuit of something, but he came back immediately when Tom whistled.

There were deer at the pond when we came out of the woods, three of them. They raised their heads, ears flicking, and they studied us anxiously. Tom took hold of Troy's collar. For ten or fifteen seconds, the deer watched us. Then all three of them leaped at the same instant and ran toward the trees at the far end of the field. The ducks took flight, squawking in outrage.

"See?" Tom said, looking after the deer. He put his hand on my shoulder. "I told you that deer came here."

The warmth from his hand seemed to burn through my shirt. I would have liked to reach up and put my hand over his, but I didn't dare. Then the moment was over. He took his hand away.

"Do they ever come close to your house?" I asked. I could see the back of his house from where we stood. Crisp red-and-white-checked curtains hung in the kitchen windows.

Tom glanced in that direction, and for a moment he appeared puzzled. Then he looked away and blinked. "The deer? Oh, sure. Mom says they come close to the porch sometimes. If Troy's not around, that is. He won't hurt them, but he likes to chase everything." His hand found the dog's ears and rubbed them. Troy's tail wagged lazily.

I half expected him to invite me in to meet his parents, but he didn't. Instead, he almost seemed to hurry me away, toward the field and the short cut to the road. Maybe we both had good reasons for not wanting our families involved, but I couldn't imagine what his would be.

"Thanks for the walk," I told him.

His strange, green eyes studied my face as if he were trying to fix me in his memory. "I hope you'll come back," he said finally. "Sometimes I get lonely."

The words hung between us. I felt myself blush.

"I looked for you at school yesterday," I told him, babbling like an idiot. "But I didn't see you." I almost added that I'd asked about him, too, but that no one had ever heard about him. I was beginning to suspect that he had even fewer friends than I did.

"I left early," he began, and then he stopped. He glanced back at the house, frowning, as if he'd forgotten something.

"Well, I'll see you," I said awkwardly. Ask me not to leave, I thought fiercely. Tell me that you'll look for me at school.

"Good-bye, Keller," he said.

I turned away before he could read the disappointment on my face, and started across the field. The dry grass whispered under my sneakers. Tiny insects leaped ahead of me. A light wind was blowing now, and I could smell autumn in it.

I looked back. Tom and Troy were gone. The house seemed deserted and shabby from here, the windows blank like closed eyes.

I ran halfway home.

On Sunday afternoon, while I was helping Grandmother wash her car, Drew arrived in a pickup truck with two bikes in the back.

"Guess what?" he said to me as he leaned out the window. "Your grandmother and I are going bike riding."

"Idiot!" Grandmother said as she casually flicked the hose in his direction, spattering him with water.

"Don't get water on Dad's truck!" Drew shouted. "It's the dirt on it that holds it together. Just for that I'm taking Keller out riding instead."

I hadn't done much bike riding, and we hadn't finished washing the car yet. I looked doubtfully at Grandmother.

"Go ahead," she said. "Drew will finish up for me when the two of you get back."

"Impossible," Drew said as he hopped out of the truck. "I have a rare tropical disease that prevents me from

washing cars today. However, if you can wait until tomorrow . . ." He grinned at Grandmother and she
laughed.

Drew let down the tailgate and pulled out both bikes.
"Pick one, Keller."

"Where'd you get them?" I asked.

"I happened to notice them in someone's garage as I
was driving past."

"Drew!" Grandmother said sharply. "You're scaring her."

I was getting a little nervous. Sometimes Drew's sense
of humor bordered on the downright peculiar.

"One bike's mine, the other belongs to Granny," Drew
began.

"Drew." Grandmother aimed the hose at his feet.

"It belongs to my mother," he said, laughing and
dancing around in the spatters. "Honest! She's a fitness
nut. She rides the bike all over town and my dad drives
along beside her in the car, eating French fries."

I looked at Grandmother for confirmation.

"It's true," she said. "Go on, Keller. Biking must
be easier than walking for miles. Just don't stay away
too long."

"I'm on an errand of mercy," Drew said, "so we'll
be back within an hour."

"What errand of mercy?" I asked as we pedaled away.

Steering with one hand, Drew pulled a small card-
board container out of his jacket pocket. "Ant eggs. I
thought I'd give the goldfish one more treat before
winter."

My heart leaped. Maybe we'd see Tom. I bent over

the handlebars and pedaled faster. The blacktop road unrolled like a ribbon under me.

When the pond came in sight, I braked. "Where shall we leave the bikes?"

"This is a first-class operation, so we'll go up the driveway and leave our bikes there," Drew said, wheeling past me.

We crested the low hill and there was a driveway, overgrown with grass. A rotting wood fence sagged beside it. Beyond, almost hidden by trees, the house presented its sad blank windows to us.

"We'd better tell them what we're doing," I said. "They won't want strangers wandering all over the place."

Drew propped his bike against a fence post that leaned a little more under the weight. "You worry too much. Look at that house. It has to be deserted."

I left the bike and followed him across the field toward the pond, but I looked back a dozen times, expecting to see Tom's mother come out and ask us who we were and what we wanted. In spite of what Drew said, I knew someone lived there.

Drew reached the pond first, and stood on a rock over the place where flat, dark green lily pads trembled on the water. He pulled out the ant eggs and scattered them. Immediately dozens of goldfish drifted up from deep water and began feasting. Some of them were at least six inches long.

"These were your pet fish?" I asked, amazed. "They're enormous."

"They were only about an inch long when I put them

in the pond," Drew said. "Actually, they weren't my pets. I saw them in the discount store in North Grange and felt sorry for them. The fish tank was dirty and they were up near the top trying to breathe. So I bought them all and brought them here."

"How often do you come out to feed them?" And how can you not know Tom? I wondered. The two of you have something in common — you really care about living things.

Drew shrugged. "I don't come out very often anymore. The fish get all the food they need in the pond. But sometimes I like to look at them. And I thought you would, too."

When the last ant egg was gone, the fish disappeared. "This is a wonderful place," I said. "I saw deer here yesterday morning."

"Deer? Are you kidding?"

"I saw three deer at the pond, on the other side. They ran off into the woods."

Drew looked toward the woods, puzzled. "If you saw 'em, you saw 'em," he said, "but I didn't think there were deer here anymore."

"I know the boy who lives here, and he sees them all the time," I said.

Drew looked at the house, frowning faintly. "I'm sure this place is deserted. Maybe you shouldn't talk to the guy when you're out here by yourself," he said.

"Why not?" I protested. "He's nice. His name is Tom Hurley and he goes to our school."

Drew shook his head. "No. I know everybody at Cascade."

I must have looked upset, because Drew added, "Maybe he goes to North Grange. He might. Some kids transfer there because they teach things Cascade doesn't." But he glanced back at the house speculatively, as if he believed it was empty.

I thought of dragging him over and knocking on the door, just to prove he was wrong. But what was I supposed to say then? Hello, Mrs. Hurley. My friend doesn't believe you live here, and I only wanted to show him that you did?

If Tom came out, that would solve everything. But Tom didn't, the house continued to look empty, and the wind was getting colder.

"We'd better go back," Drew said.

"Sure." I looked back at the pond. A movement in the trees startled me, and for a second I thought I saw Troy there. But I was mistaken. I ran after Drew and didn't mention Tom again that day.

My parents called me that night. They'd had a serious offer for our house in Seattle and hoped that the place would be sold soon. "We'll be there by Christmas," Mom said. "Dad's new job will be waiting for him, we'll find our own house, and we'll all get healthy in that good country air."

She meant that I'd get healthy. There wasn't anything wrong with them. They had to move away from the city because of my health. They never blamed me, but I did. Sick people spoil everything for everybody.

"You're taking care of yourself, aren't you?" Mom asked. "No more problems like the one you had the other night?"

"No more," I said. "You know how it goes. I'll be sick one night and great for weeks after that." That wasn't exactly true, but my mother let me tell little stories like that.

"Okay, I'll call again in a few days," she said. "Take care. We love you."

As soon as I hung up, I surrendered to the tightness in my chest that had been building and building since Drew and I were at the pond. I pulled out my inhaler.

When Rose called me a few minutes later, Grandmother told her I was in the shower and would call her back. I was surprised at what a good liar she was.

"Thanks," I gasped. I was leaning forward over the table, supporting myself by my arms.

Grandmother patted my shoulder, then clasped her arms over her chest, hugging herself. "Should I take you back to the hospital? Should I call the doctor?"

I shook my head without speaking.

"Do you want one of those sedatives?" she asked. "The doctor said you should take one if you get bad."

I hated the sedatives, but I hated ending up in the emergency room, too. I nodded and Grandmother brought the bottle of capsules and a glass of water. I couldn't get the lid off the bottle, so she took it. Self-hatred brought tears to my eyes.

Grandmother handed me the capsule and the glass. I washed the sedative down. Tears dripped off my chin.

"I'm sorry," I gasped.

"Please don't apologize," Grandmother said. "It breaks my heart."

She looked at her watch. "I'm giving this a half hour

41

more, and if you aren't better, I'm taking you back to the emergency room for one of those injections."

I nodded. But in a half hour, I was better, and a few minutes later I went to bed, to sleep like a zombie for half the night. I didn't think of Rose until dawn.

Oh well, I told myself, when I remembered her call. It was just a matter of time until she got tired of me. I rolled over and cried myself back to sleep.

Five

I went to school on Monday in spite of Grandmother's misgivings. Crawling back in bed would have been easier, but I knew from experience that if I indulged myself even a little bit, getting dressed on Tuesday would be that much harder.

When I was still in grade school, Dr. Mercer told me I had to learn to be tough with myself. "Don't give in, Keller," he said. "Learn to fight back. You could outgrow your allergies, but you might not be able to outgrow being a loser." I'd hated him when I was a kid, until one night in the hospital I woke up and found him sitting by my bed with his hands over his face. He didn't know that I saw him cry, but after that, I loved him.

In art class, I apologized to Rose for not calling her back. "Something came up," I told her.

She shrugged. "It wasn't important. I just wanted to talk."

She didn't seem offended, but I was tempted to ex-

43

plain that I'd been sick. Miss Penny, the teacher, came around then, so I had a chance to think the whole thing over while she looked at my drawing. By the time she moved on to someone else, I decided that I'd better not say anything and let Rose think whatever she wanted to think. I knew all the ways to keep a safe distance between me and everyone else. Confiding in people wasn't one of those ways.

At lunch we both sat at Drew's table. The chair next to his was empty again, so it seemed that either the kids were taking it for granted that I was Drew's new girl or he was refusing to let anyone else sit there. Either way, there wasn't anything I could do without making a scene. I put my tray down and nodded to him.

"Keller, love, when are you going to answer today's question?" he said. He was eating a slice of pizza and didn't look up at me.

In first period, he'd asked me if I wanted to go bike riding that afternoon. The teacher had interrupted by asking him to put his social life on hold and pay attention to class. I'd been grateful then, but now I had to respond.

"Are you going to feed your fish again?" I asked.

"No, I was thinking about feeding you," he said. "How about a hot fudge sundae after school?"

My mouth watered instantly, but chocolate was on my poison list. "I can't go this afternoon," I told him. "Maybe some other time, though." I promised myself that I was going to rehearse at least three good excuses and keep them on the tip of my tongue.

"We could go riding and skip the sundae," Drew said. "I know that you girls are always dieting."

"That's not it." I busied myself with my sandwich, rearranging the lettuce before I bit into it. "I've already got plans that I can't change." Such as washing my hair and sewing a button on my yellow shirt, I thought.

He sighed melodramatically. "Well, guys," he said to the rest of the kids at the table, "what am I going to do with her? No matter what I offer her — rubies, pearls, fast cars — she keeps on turning me down."

Everybody laughed, including me. But Drew's mouth was vulnerable and hurt. He saw me watching him and he looked away, smiled suddenly, and looked back. "Did I ever tell you how much I like red hair?" he asked. "It turns me on."

I poked his arm. "Quit that."

He did. He didn't talk to me again that day, and when I passed him in the halls, he smiled vaguely at me, as if he'd forgotten my name but didn't care enough to ask me to tell him again. I pushed my disappointment away, into a back corner of my mind where it joined a lot of other disappointments. People always seemed to end up hurting each other for one reason or another.

The day grew warmer as it went along, and by the time I got off the school bus that afternoon, I was so hot that I carried my jacket. But there were fat piles of dark clouds waiting on the horizon. I quickened my step. I wanted to walk to the pond again, but Grandmother would forbid it if rain was already falling.

She was in the kitchen, and when I walked in, she

said, "I worried all day. I expected a call from the nurse any minute."

"I feel great," I said. "Honestly." I was afraid that she was regretting letting me stay with her until my parents moved. It wasn't that she didn't love me. It was that I caused a lot of anxiety. I hated knowing that. I couldn't bear watching people wondering how long it would be before I had another bad time and scared them — and myself — and needed to see the doctor right away or go to the hospital.

"Can I do something for you?" I asked. "Do you need some errands run? Can I help with the house-work?"

But Grandmother said, "No. You rest for a while or watch TV." She smiled reluctantly. "Or go for one of those walks of yours."

"I'll walk," I said, and I hurried away before she could tell me again what a dangerous idea she thought it was.

There were more black clouds on the horizon when I came out of the house. I could feel the weather change coming, and I hoped it would hold off long enough for me to get to the pond and back. I hurried along the road, wishing I had my own bike. Well, why not? I could ask Mom when she called. Bike rides in the country air sounded healthy. She ought to like the idea.

Before the pond came into sight, I stopped and used my inhaler. No one saw me except a jay preening him-self on a fence post. He didn't care what I did as long as I got moving again.

I didn't see Tom at first, and I was so disappointed

46

that my feet dragged. The black clouds were boiling closer now. I felt threatened.

But then Tom came out out of the woods with Troy behind him, and he called my name. I was unable to hide my joy.

"I wasn't sure you'd come back," he said. "Troy and I keep looking for you, though."

He seemed nervous, tucking in his white shirt and rolling the sleeves back a little more. When his eyes finally met mine, he looked at me almost too long. We both glanced away at the same time.

I half expected him to say that he'd seen Drew and me feeding the fish in the pond. When he didn't, I said, "I was here with a friend named Drew. He's the one who put the goldfish in the pond, and he brought food for them."

"I didn't know there were goldfish here."

I wondered why he didn't ask me about Drew. He didn't seem to have any real curiosity about the goldfish either. He kept looking over at his house, as if he expected someone to come out.

"Are you busy? Would you rather I went home?" I asked reluctantly.

"No," he said hastily, and he grabbed my hand. "Don't go. I was waiting for you to show up here again, and I don't want you to leave yet."

"Then what's wrong?" I asked. "You act as if you're worried about something."

He shook his head. "No. It's just that sometimes . . . Never mind." He laughed. "Don't pay any attention to me. I've been worried about Troy's foot, I guess."

"But he seems better," I said. "He hardly limps at all now, do you, Troy?" The dog, hearing me say his name, wagged his tail.

But Tom wasn't satisfied. "I wish it hadn't happened. It shouldn't have happened."

"I hope the boy who put the trap there is sorry," I said.

"I haven't seen him since that day," Tom said. "Look, let's not talk about sad things. Would you like to go through the woods to the cliff?"

"Sure." I was so busy hoping he wouldn't let go of my hand that I hadn't noticed that the clouds had retreated to the horizon again, and the wind that ruffled our hair was warm, a summer wind, with no hint of autumn in it. "I'd love to do that."

"Come on," Tom said, and we turned toward the path in the woods. He kept my hand in his, and my fingers gripped his tightly.

This is stupid and I'm going to be sorry, I told myself. But he'd seen me sick and he never mentioned it again. Maybe it wouldn't be a problem between us. Maybe he wouldn't be embarrassed if I had trouble breathing when we were out somewhere.

Oh, sure, I thought. And while I'm daydreaming, why don't I just pretend that I'm never sick at all. That would solve everything.

The sun beat down on the flat rock where we sat, and I soaked up the heat gratefully. Troy lay with his head in my lap, and I fingered his collar lazily. Two metal disks were fastened on a ring near the buckle. Troy's name was engraved on the round one, and there was a

48

number on the oval disk — his dog license, probably.

Troy shook his head impatiently and moved a few inches from me.

Tom laughed. "He doesn't like it when someone touches his collar. I guess his tags are like jewelry to him."

I laughed, too, and wished Tom would take my hand again.

"This is a great place to watch the sunset," he said. "The tops of the trees look like they're on fire then."

I wondered if he usually came to the cliffs alone, but I couldn't ask that, so we sat in silence for a long time. Silences didn't seem to bother him. He sat with his eyes closed, his dark lashes casting shadows on his cheeks, and he smiled.

But I needed him to talk now. I wanted to know everything about him. "What grade are you in?" I asked.

He opened his eyes and for a moment, I thought he was surprised to see me there. "What? Oh, I'm a senior."

"What will you do after high school? Are you going to college?"

"I have to go in the military first," he said, as if that was something he was taking for granted. "Then I'll go to college."

"What will you take? What are you going to do when you're out of college?" I wondered even as I asked how anyone could make plans that far ahead. I certainly couldn't.

"I want to do something with animals," he said. "I don't know what. Maybe work in a zoo." He laughed,

49

embarrassed. "It's probably interesting only to me," he said. "But I generally like animals better than people."

I wasn't sure how to take that. "Animals are pretty nice," I said feebly.

"Hey," he said, and he reached for my hand. "Don't you know what I mean?"

His smile told me what he meant. I gripped his hand hard and leaned my head back again and shut my eyes. "I know," I said.

"Sometimes I feel lonely," he said quietly, "but not for people. I don't want a crowd around me, with everybody talking at once. That doesn't make me happy. I'm not sure what does make me happy — oh, being here, I guess. Or spending time with Troy. Or spending time with someone like you. I don't mean that I don't like to talk to people. It's just that I've always felt as if I were talking to shadows. Or maybe I'm the shadow and they're the ones who are real."

"With me it's a little different." I realized that I was about to trust him with my biggest secret and I didn't feel the least bit afraid. "I don't feel safe with people. I'm never sure when I'm going to have another asthma attack and be embarrassed. I can tell that most people really want to take off running when I get sick. They hope I'll disappear and when I don't, they wish they could. Once, when I was in the hospital, I had a roommate who was epileptic. She told me that's how people felt about her, too."

"Maybe everyone gets scared when they see sick people."

"You didn't get scared," I said.

"No. Maybe I had all my fears burned out of me when Troy got his foot caught in that trap. I was so scared then that for a moment I almost gave up and left him under the water. The trap was so strong — I got out of breath so fast."

"But you got him free."

"Yes."

We sat quietly then, watching the sun slide down the sky. It occurred to me that what'd I'd said to him wasn't exactly true anymore. I didn't feel threatened by everyone. Here I was, friends with Tom. Rose might be safe, too, although I couldn't be sure yet. And sometimes I thought that Drew was determined to be a friend, even if I tried to discourage him.

"Do you like to read?" Tom asked suddenly.

"Yes. I even like poetry."

Tom grinned. "I like the kind that rhymes."

"You like the kind that's hard to write."

"Do you write poetry?" he asked eagerly.

I shook my head. "I've tried but I'm terrible. What poets do you like best?"

He thought. "Walter de la Mare's my favorite."

"I like Kipling. Not the poems about India as much as some of the others. 'The Way Through the Woods' and the one about the war between the gods. The words to that one are so beautiful that I memorized the whole thing."

"Tell it to me," he said.

I shook my head. "I'd get nervous and forget a line."

"I wouldn't mind," Tom said earnestly, "not even if you had to start all over again the way I do. Once when

51

I was trying to say de la Mare's 'The Listeners,' I had to start twice. The class didn't really want to hear it anyway. But I want to hear you.''

"Nope. You get the book of Kipling's poems from the school library. Ask Mrs. Mannerly for it.''

"Who? The librarian's name is North,'' Tom said.

That perplexed me. I'd been certain she was called Mannerly.

"I'll get the book soon,'' Tom said. "It's nice talking to someone who does something besides listen to the radio.''

"Or watch situation comedies,'' I added.

"What? Oh. I don't see many movies,'' Tom said.

"I love even silly movies,'' I confessed. We laughed together until Troy raised his head and stared at us.

I didn't want to leave, but I'd stayed too long already. Tom made it easy for me to forget time.

"You have to go,'' he said quietly, looking at me.

"Yes.'' I stood up, and Troy, alert, leaped up beside me, his collar jingling.

"But you'll be back?'' he asked.

"Yes.'' Suddenly I wanted him to come home with me. I'd tell Grandmother that we met by the pond, not in it, and hope she didn't ask where he lived.

"Can you come back with me and meet my grandmother?'' I asked. It'll work out, I told myself desperately. I'll make it work out.

But he had that puzzled expression again. "I'm sorry,'' he said, "but I have to go home myself. There's something . . . well, I have to go.''

He'd stood up and was looking out over the forest

below us. I had the momentary, and terrifying, impression that Tom had already left, that what I was looking at was only the memory of him, captured by the light of the late afternoon sun and evaporating even as I watched.

He didn't take my hand again. He walked so fast that I had trouble keeping up with him. "Tom, what's wrong?" I asked.

We were at the edge of the woods. He stopped and looked down at me.

"What's wrong?" I repeated.

He looked over at his house. The kitchen curtains were blowing. In the distance, thunder growled.

"You'd better hurry," he said. "It's going to rain."

Troy ran off toward the house, then looked back and barked.

"Will you be here the next time I come?" I asked fearfully. Something was happening that I didn't understand.

He grabbed me by my shoulders. "I'll try," he said, and he bent his head and kissed me once, hard, then pulled me close to his chest. "Don't be afraid, Keller."

"I won't," I promised, not even knowing what he meant.

He let go of me and started toward the house. Troy barked again, sharply, as if saying, "Hurry!"

"I'll see you, Keller."

"Good-bye, Tom!" I didn't wait until he went inside, but hurried around the pond toward the field. When I reached the road, I looked back. The house seemed empty. Overhead, thunder rolled across a darkening sky.

The storm had come so fast it frightened me, and I ran toward home.

I reached my grandmother's house just as the first drops of rain fell. She was sitting in the living room, under a lamp, reading a book. "Well, that was a fast walk," she said. "Did the rain chase you home?"

"Just about," I said. Good. She'd lost track of time and didn't know how long I'd been gone.

I climbed the stairs, examining a new thought. Time keeps us prisoners. We ought to be brave enough to forget about clocks and calendars and just go ahead and live our lives.

I wondered what Tom would think of a strange idea like that.

Six

In art class the next day, Miss Penny asked us to draw a scene we remembered that had both a person and an animal in it. Without stopping to plan, I sketched Tom leaning against the rock, with Troy sleeping next to him.

"Hey," Rose said, "that's wonderful."

I blinked and looked up at her. "How long have you been standing there?"

"Since forever, that's all. You were really concentrating." She turned the sketch so that she could see it better. "Who is this?"

"Tom Hurley."

"The boy you saw out by Deerfield Pond? And this is his dog?"

"Troy. The dog caught his foot in a beaver trap in the pond and Tom rescued him. Troy still has a limp, but his foot's getting better."

Rose looked from the sketch to me and back to the

sketch again. "I never heard of trappers at that pond. In fact, I didn't even know there were beavers there. That's awful. Poor dog."

I turned the sketch to face me again. I didn't want to talk to Rose about Tom anymore. She might ask questions and I didn't have any answers. But that doesn't matter, I thought fiercely. Tom is Tom. He doesn't need to be explained.

"Do you see him very often?" Rose asked, but tactfully she avoided looking directly at me.

"I only see him once in a while," I said. Why doesn't she go back to her own drawing board? I could feel my skin prickle and knew I was blushing.

Thoughts rattled around in my head like pebbles in a can. What if she wanted to meet Tom? What if she went out to the pond by herself and Tom wasn't there? She'd think I was crazy, because the house looked vacant from the road. It wasn't until you got around in back and saw the curtains in the windows that you realized someone lived there.

"Drew likes you a lot," Rose said quietly.

"He hardly knows me," I told her. Miss Penny was wandering down our row, spending a little time with each student. Hurry, I thought. Rose will leave if you hurry and start talking to me.

"You don't have to know people very well to like them," Rose said. "Maybe, if you're sort of going with this Tom, you ought to say something to Drew before he starts caring too much."

I looked up at her, astonished. "I've known Drew Sennett about one week," I said. "He can't be serious."

56

"You've only known this Tom for a week and you're serious," Rose said. She pointed her pencil at my drawing. "You are absolutely crazy about him."

Impulsively, I turned the drawing over so she couldn't see it.

"Don't be mad at me," Rose whispered urgently, her gaze following Miss Penny's progress. "I know how you feel. But Drew's my friend. Understand?"

I nodded, anxious for her to move away. When she did, I turned the drawing face up and looked at it for signs of my feelings. I saw nothing but Tom resting against a rock with his dog by his side.

"That's remarkable," Miss Penny said over my shoulder. "You have a gift for portraits. I'd like to see what you do in oils someday."

She passed by me, smiling. Shakily, I rubbed one hand over my forehead. Had she seen my secret, too?

I looked out the window at the windswept sky, knowing that I loved the strange boy who'd saved me from drowning. I also knew that loving Tom was like loving the cloud shadows that were racing over the distant hills. Somehow, I wasn't certain why, Tom was out of my reach. Even when he kissed me, he was out of reach.

After school, I went to the pond again, determined that this time I was going to ask more questions. Tom, I would say, where do you go to school? Can I meet your mother today? Will you come to my house for dinner soon?

He wasn't at the pond and I didn't see him at the edge of the woods. The house seemed empty, as it always did, but I walked toward it anyway, heading toward the back where the red-and-white curtains hung in the windows.

The curtains were gone. The windows were blank, reflecting the cold gray light from the overcast sky. A morning glory vine with yellowing leaves straggled across the porch.

I took a deep breath and climbed the wooden steps. "Tom?" I called out. "Are you home?"

I thought I heard a faint sigh from inside the house. "Tom? Mrs. Hurley?" I shouted. "Can you hear me?"

No one answered, so I raised my fist and knocked on the door, gently at first and then harder and harder, until my knuckles stung. No one came. The only sound I heard was the wind in the poplar trees on the other side of the house.

I left then, embarrassed, wondering if someone was inside, listening to the racket I'd raised and wishing I'd go away and not come back.

Ducks were paddling on the pond again, a dozen of them at least. While I watched, they took wing, circled once, and turned south.

Winter's coming, I thought. My loneliness overwhelmed me and I bit my lip. Perhaps Tom was at his favorite place on the cliff. But I couldn't go there alone and intrude on his privacy.

I walked slowly down the driveway, trying not to cry. I didn't understand anything. Had I really seen curtains in the kitchen windows before? Perhaps Tom's family didn't live there and I had somehow misunderstood him.

No. I was certain about the curtains.

Take one day at a time, my favorite doctor had told

me once. Don't waste your energy worrying about what's going to happen tomorrow. And whatever happens to-day — well, go with it, Keller.

I remembered the day Dr. Mercer had told me that. He'd had asthma worse than I did, and on that day he'd also had a terrible rash on his face. "I'm allergic to my new allergy pills," he'd told me, laughing.

A few days later he had a massive coronary during an asthma attack and died in the hospital the next morning. I got so sick the day he died that I ended up in the hospital, too.

I never had another doctor who sat by my bed.

Remembering him cost me my appetite and I only picked at my dinner. Afterward I fell asleep in my room with the light on and a book open on my chest. At dawn I woke suddenly, certain that I'd heard a dog bark close by, a collar jingle.

I went to the window, but nothing was there.

"Troy?" I whispered.

In the distance, far down Birch road, I heard Troy's faint bark. I closed the window and went back to bed, happy.

Tom was back.

Seven

I wanted to go to the pond the next afternoon, but when I got home from school, Grandmother surprised me with the news that a friend of hers was going to drive us to North Grange in her pickup truck and bring home a bike for me.

"Although," Grandmother added unhappily, "I hope you won't ever go riding alone. It would be so dangerous for you."

"But Mom and Dad said it was okay for me to have a bike," I reminded her. I had to work hard not to cheer. This meant I could get to the pond faster and stay longer.

Grandmother's friend, Mrs. Ashburn, was late. I was so impatient I could scarely keep my feet still. When we were finally on our way, Mrs. Ashburn decided that she ought to make a slight detour so that she could show Grandmother a house that had just been put up for sale.

"Your son and his family might like this," she said

as she slowed down in front of a large house on the opposite side of Cascade from Grandmother's. "It needs repairs, but I heard that the owner is eager to sell, so the price is reasonable."

I longed to cry out, "Never mind the house! Let's get the bike!" But I tried to pretend an interest in the house because Grandmother was so excited.

"It seems to have possibilities," she said. "And it's close enough to the high school so that Keller can walk."

"It's six blocks away," Mrs. Ashburn said.

"What do you think?" Grandmother asked me.

My brain finally registered the conversation. She was serious about this house. "It looks fine, Grandmother, but isn't it pretty far away from you?" I really meant that the house was far away from the pond, but that wasn't a smart thing to say.

"It's about two miles," Mrs. Ashburn said. "A nice bike ride."

"Hmm." Grandmother wasn't sure if she liked that idea.

"We'll see what Mom and Dad think," I said. "Maybe we should get going now."

Mrs. Ashburn laughed and turned back to the main road. "We'll be home with your bike in less than an hour, Keller," she said.

But we weren't home in an hour. It was close to dinner time when Mrs. Ashburn finally dropped us off. I wanted desperately to ride to the pond, but Grandmother insisted that we eat before I leave, and that took forever.

I loaded the dishwasher as fast as I could and ran up the back stairs two at a time. There was perhaps only an hour of daylight left, but I had the bike now, and the trip to the pond wouldn't take long. Tom would be there. He had to be there. I was sure that I'd heard Troy barking at dawn.

I was almost out the door when Grandmother called me back.

"You aren't going far, are you?" she asked. "It's going to be dark soon."

"I'm just going down the road a little way," I told her. "The bike's wonderful, Grandmother, and I can't wait to try it out. I'll be right back."

She was going to say something else, but the phone rang, and while she was talking to a friend from church, I escaped.

I felt as if I were flying. The long, empty road invited me to fling myself forward. The wind in my face exhilarated me and I laughed aloud.

I left my bike leaning against a post by Tom's driveway. The house was silent, closed in upon itself. I shouted Tom's name, and was rewarded only with a burst of complaint from several crows across the road.

The pond looked far away across the field, a trick of the evening light. I started toward it. "Tom!" I shouted. "Are you here?"

Troy barked. Tom and the dog were standing near the woods. Tom waved and walked toward me.

We met at the pond and stood there awkwardly. I wondered if he remembered kissing me — and if he hoped that I'd remember.

"I looked for you yesterday but you weren't here," I said.

He reached down and touched Troy's head, as if for reassurance. "I didn't see you," he said.

"How's Troy's foot?" I asked, for something to say. The dog looked fine, but Tom kept his hand on him, as if he was worried.

"It's still a little sore," Tom said.

My mouth was dry. I was having trouble keeping up the conversation. Tom seemed — tired, maybe. I wasn't certain he was happy that I'd come.

"It's cool tonight," I said finally. "I'm glad I wore my heavy jacket. Aren't you cold?" Tom wasn't wearing anything over his white shirt.

He glanced down at his shirt as if he'd forgotten what he was wearing. "I'm fine," he said. "Have you been taking care of yourself?"

"Sure. I've got a bike now. It doesn't take me as long to get here. Do you have a bike?" We could go riding, I thought.

"Bike?" he said, and he looked back at the house. "It's not here, I guess."

Silence. He didn't explain why his bike wasn't there. Perhaps he didn't really like bikes. Maybe he had his own car, but where? How did he get to school in North Grange?

"Let's sit down by the pond," he said quietly. "Sometimes the quail come by before dark. The young ones are almost as big as their parents now."

We sat on a rock by the water, waiting. After a while Tom reached for my hand. "Maybe they've already been here," he said.

"Did you see the deer today?" I asked.

He seemed to be trying to remember. Finally, he said, "Yes. They were eating apples from the tree behind the house."

"I wish I'd seen that," I said wistfully.

The light was leaving the sky gently, fading in the east, flowing in the west like liquid mother-of-pearl. Troy sighed and dropped his head to his paws. Wind hissed in the tops of the poplar trees on the other side of the house.

"I think about you a lot," Tom said. He didn't look at me, though. His gaze was fixed on the pond.

"I think about you, too," I said shakily.

There were a hundred questions I wanted to ask him, but I was afraid of the answers I'd get. Don't think about anything except being here, I told myself. Don't spoil this.

Would I dare to lean against his arm? Would he like it?

"Keller," he said at the same moment I said "Tom."

We both laughed, and he slid his arm around me easily. "When I first saw you swimming, do you know what I thought?"

I blushed and turned my face away so he couldn't see. "I suppose you wondered who was swimming in your pond in her shirt."

He pulled me closer. "That, too. But first, I thought you were some sort of illusion. Someone from a fairy tale."

"With red hair?" I asked, laughing.

He leaned his cheek against my hair. "Why not? I'd never seen a girl swimming in the pond, so it took me a minute to realize that you were real. And then I saw you getting into trouble.''

I turned my face to his chest. "Don't talk about it. I can't stand to remember.''

"Then we'll just remember the first part — me standing there watching a red-haired girl floating on the water and grinning.''

"Was I grinning?" I asked, delighted at the idea.

"Oh, yes," he said. "You looked so happy that I grinned myself. I wanted to get in the water and find out what you thought was so wonderful. But I remembered the traps and then you — "

"Don't," I said quickly, and I put my hand up to touch his lips and seal them.

He kissed my fingers. I moved my hand to touch his face, his hair. When I looked up, he bent his head and kissed me.

He was the only boy who had ever kissed me. I had never even had what could be called a romantic date. Loving a boy wasn't something I'd wanted to risk trying. I was sure that sooner or later he'd see me sick and he'd either be disgusted or laugh. I couldn't decide which was worse.

Once, when I was in the eighth grade, a girl named Darla Sessions invited me to her New Year's Eve party. She didn't especially want me there, but she wanted to be able to say that fifty kids showed up for her party. I went, though. At one point, when everyone was dancing and no one had asked me, I crept into a corner by one of the snack tables, trying to be invisible. Bernie Wise swaggered over. He'd been the biggest bully in grade school and in junior high he was an overbearing creep who threw rocks at dogs and had been suspended twice for drinking beer in the gym locker room.

He stuffed his mouth full of candy and stared at me. "What are you looking at, Wheezy?" he said. "If you think I'll dance with you, forget it."

I went home then, walking alone in the dark, with my fists clenched in my pockets, and I never forgot his contemptuous look.

If a boy I hated could hurt me, how much pain could a boy I liked cause me? I pulled free of Tom's arms. But it was already too late, because I could almost feel my heart breaking.

"I'm sorry," Tom said quickly. "I shouldn't have done that."

I covered my face with my hands. "I wanted you to, but it's not a good idea."

"Why not? Is it me? You don't like me?"

I dropped my hands and faced him. "It's not that. It's just that I'd better not get involved with anyone."

He looked at me with such dismay that tears spurted into my eyes. "My grandmother wouldn't like it," I babbled, not being able to think of anything else. And then, afraid that he might think Grandmother would be set against him without even meeting him, I shook my head violently and blurted, "No, that's not it. It's because I'm sick so much."

"You mean the way you were the day I found you in the pond? But that doesn't happen very often, does it? And I'd never do what you said other people do — run away from you."

"I've been in the hospital a lot of times."

He was watching me while I talked, and I had to look away.

"Isn't there medicine you can take?" he asked.

"Sure. But it doesn't cure it. It just helps me for a while. And sometimes it doesn't help very much."

"That's awful," he said, and he reached for me, pulling me close to him. "I'm sorry. I didn't know it was so bad. You shouldn't come here, then. It's too far. You must get tired out. If I'd known — "

"Would you have come to my house?" I asked, afraid of what his answer would be.

He was silent for a long time. I sat up straight, pushing his arms away. I had to bite my lower lip to keep it from trembling.

"I'd try," he said and his voice broke.

I stared at him. "What do you mean, try?" I asked, suddenly cold and afraid.

He started to say something, then changed his mind.

"What?" I demanded. "What is it?"

"Sometimes — well, I can't always get away. Things come up."

I didn't understand him. "What do you mean?"

He shook his head slowly. "I'm not sure I know."

"You're scaring me," I said. "Are you in some kind of trouble?"

But he didn't answer my question. He stood up suddenly and helped me to my feet. "It's almost dark," he said. "You'd better start home."

"Tom — " I began.

"You have to go," he said. He pulled me a few steps

until I stopped resisting and walked with him. He held my hand tightly. He brought it to his lips and kissed my palm.

"What's wrong?" I whispered.

"Nothing," he said. "But you have to go now."

"Will you come with me part of the way?"

We were standing beside my bike then. "I can't," he whispered. "I'm sorry."

I thought I could see a faint light in his house, but I wasn't certain. Did his parents sit in the dark? Perhaps they were watching television. Would they be angry if he went partway home with me?

"Okay," I said. I turned my face up so that he'd kiss me.

"When will you come back?" he whispered.

"Tomorrow," I said. "No, wait! I'm not sure I can. I have to go to North Grange to see my doctor tomorrow."

"The day after tomorrow," he said.

"Yes," I whispered against his neck.

I rode away in the dark. Grandmother was angry when I got home. My excuse — that I'd gotten lost on a side road — only made her angrier.

"You can't take chances like that," she said. "What if you'd had one of your attacks?"

I hated those words. *One* of *your* attacks. "Well, I didn't," I said. "I'm terribly sorry you were worried. I feel wonderful. The bike is going to be good for me."

"Not if you stay out in the dark," she said.

I smiled apologetically at her and would have escaped

upstairs then, but she told me I'd had two phone calls. Rose wanted me to call back, but Drew had only wanted to say hello.

I phoned Rose. "Sorry I'm calling back so late," I said. "I was out for a while."

"With Tom Hurley?" she asked.

I hesitated, and before I could speak, she said, "I'm sorry, Keller. You don't have to answer that. It's none of my business."

"It's all right." I glanced around to see where Grandmother was. She'd gone into the living room and was looking through the television program guide. "I did see Tom," I said softly. "But I'm back now. What do you want?"

"I thought it might be fun if we did something after school tomorrow," Rose said. "We could go shopping here or in North Grange, or just go for a nice long walk. How about it?"

"Sorry. I've got something I have to do tomorrow," I said. "I'd like to go shopping with you sometime," I added. I didn't want to hurt her.

"What do you have to do tomorrow? I'm getting my mom's car. I could take you."

Inwardly, I sighed. I was going to have to work on that list of excuses. "I've got an appointment with a doctor," I said.

Rose giggled. "Gee, Keller, I go to the doctor once in a while myself, so I'm not blown away by the news. How about I take you and wait for you? We can still go shopping afterward."

69

"My appointment isn't until four-thirty in North Grange. I always have to wait, so I might not be out before five-thirty."

"There are all sorts of stores open until nine," she said. "Hey, I 've got a terrific idea. Why don't we have dinner together before we go shopping? I'd have you home in plenty of time to do your homework, if that's what's worrying you."

Well, why not go? I asked myself. If I went with Grandmother, we wouldn't be back until six. She'd insist that I eat dinner before I went out and then we'd be back to arguing about my riding the bike so close to dark. There wasn't much chance that I'd be seeing Tom tomorrow anyway.

"That sounds nice," I told Rose.

"Are you going to see that allergy specialist in North Grange?" she asked. "Dr. Jacoby?"

"That's the one," I said. "Do you know him?"

"He's my mom's doctor," she told me. "Remember, I told you she had asthma, too?"

"I remember. How is she?"

"She doesn't have much trouble with it," Rose said. "She says getting older makes one problem better and six others worse."

"Oh, wonderful," I said bitterly. "I'm afraid to even think about what I've got in store for me after this."

"Sorry!" Rose said. "I didn't mean to upset you. Listen, now I'll tell you something to cheer you up."

"Okay, go ahead," I said.

"Drew told me that he wants to ask you to the first school dance we have."

"I'd really rather he didn't," I said hastily. "If he says anything more to you about it, try to discourage him."

"But why?" Rose demanded. "He's lots of fun. And unless you're actually going steady with that Tom, can't you give Drew a chance?"

"I don't go to dances," I said.

"Or you don't go to dances unless Tom asks you," Rose said.

"Not that. I just don't go."

Rose was silent for a moment. "I wish I could change your mind," she said finally. And then she told me good-bye and hung up.

The call left me feeling vaguely uncomfortable, as if I were being drawn into all sorts of involvements that I wasn't ready for yet.

Eight

On Thursday, Rose waited for me while Dr. Jacoby listened to me breathe, said "Hmm," and wrote out new prescriptions for the medicines I used. When I came out of his examining room, she said, "How did it go?"

"The same as it always goes," I said. "But listen, that's not important. Where are we going to eat?"

Rose shoved open the clinic door and held it for me. "There's a great hamburger place in North Grange. We all go there. You'll love it." She looked at my face. "Really. You'll have a great time."

The restaurant wasn't far away and it was already jammed with people, but Rose found room for us at a small table squeezed in next to a long table where a dozen kids yelled her name and waved. She left me while she went to the counter for our order. The kids looked at me curiously and I pretended that I didn't notice.

When Rose came back, she introduced me. The kids

were from North Grange, and I wanted to ask them if they knew Tom Hurley, but I had an awful feeling that they'd say they never heard of him and I didn't want to hear that. I didn't want any more mysteries.

Well, maybe that wasn't exactly true. When I was with Tom, the mysteries were exciting. I loved them and hated them, wanted more and dreaded them. But the longer I was away from him, the more anxious I became, and then I felt a desperate need to ask questions and get answers.

Yet there, in the restaurant, when I could have asked one question and received an answer, I refused to do it.

"Are you feeling all right?" Rose asked me, keeping her voice low.

"Sure." She surprised me. "I feel great. I'm not supposed to eat hamburgers, but sometimes I do, and this one is good."

"What are you supposed to eat?" she asked.

"Dry whole wheat toast and sprouts, with water on the side," I told her, laughing.

"You sound like Mom," Rose said. "She's not supposed to eat anything that tastes good, but she does."

When we finished eating, Rose said good-bye to her friends and we left, walking out into the cool, clear evening air. I took a deep breath.

"You still okay, Keller?"

"Fine. You don't need to keep asking me."

"You look a little tired," Rose said. "But if you're all right, let's walk up this way. There's a store here that sells the cutest shirts. Wait until you see them."

I walked patiently with her, wishing that it had somehow been possible for me to have gone out to the pond. I needed Tom. I looked up at the sky and wondered if he was thinking about me. Maybe he was looking up, too.

"Here we are," Rose said, stopping in front of a small shop. "What do you think?"

"It's great," I told her. Rose was a nice girl. No, more than nice. I hadn't had a friend for a long time. "Hey, look," I said, pointing out a pretty plaid shirt in the window. "What do you think of that?"

We went inside and I put Tom out of my mind. There was always tomorrow.

But it rained the next day, beginning around noon. By the time school was out, the streets were running with water and still the rain came down. I got wet hurrying from the school to the bus and even wetter when I got off the bus.

After dinner, I waited at my bedroom window until dark, watching the rain and wishing it would stop. Finally I gave up and sat in the living room, watching television with Grandmother.

Then the phone rang, and I answered it on the extension in the hall.

"Hello, my heart's desire."

"Drew? Is that you?" I was already starting to laugh.

"Who else? Have you been unfaithful to me with so many different guys that you don't know who's calling you his heart's desire?"

"Okay. I give up. What do you want?"

"There's a great movie at North Grange. Ask your

grandmother if you can go and tell her not to keep me waiting too long, because I'm using the phone in Dead Man's Grotto out on the highway and some weird guys are waiting in line behind me and cracking their knuckles.''

I put the phone down and went back into the living room. "Drew wants to take me to a movie," I said. I was confident that she'd say I couldn't go on such short notice.

"Good idea," she said, her eyes on the TV screen.

Dismayed at my mistake in thinking that she would give me an excuse, I went back to the phone. "I can go."

"I'll pick you up right away," Drew said. "These guys are getting closer all the time and they're arguing about who gets my genuine artificial leather watch strap."

I grinned, resigned. "I'm saving your life, I guess."

He laughed. "Not yet. But I'll show you how after the movie, when I take you out back of the stadium and let you see my tattoo."

"Oh, wonderful!" I said, falling in with his foolishness. "Grandmother will want to see that, too, so I'll bring her along." I hung up before he could answer and went upstairs for my coat.

Drew was there within ten minutes and I met him at the door. He looked different. I stared at him for a moment before I realized he wasn't wearing his glasses.

"I'm not sure I want to go with you if you can't see," I said.

"I'm wearing contacts," he told me. "I save 'em for special occasions, and this is special, since your grandmother is coming with us."

"I am not!" Grandmother shouted from the living room. "Hello and good-bye, Drew. You're interrupting my program."

Drew shut the door firmly. "Aw, heck," he said to me. "If she isn't coming, maybe I'd better just give you a map and a buck for the bus. I'm not sure I want to be alone with you."

"Quit it." I poked him gently. "Let's run for the car. I don't want to get wet again."

He grabbed my hand and we sprinted to the car. Once inside with the door closed against the downpour, I asked him where we were really going.

"To the movie," he said. "Did you think I was kidding? It's supposed to be a good one. Afterward, I'll take you to a place in North Grange that serves great peach pie. How does that sound?"

"Yum yum," I said.

"Was that in reference to me or to the pie?" Drew started the car and peered through the windshield. "What a horrible night." He looked over at me suddenly. "Come on. Was it me or the pie?"

The porch light lit up the inside of car and I saw the expression on his face. Drew was part clown. The rest of him puzzled me. "The pie sounds good," I said. I had a hard time laughing then. How serious was he?

His grin was lopsided. "Fair enough." He pulled out of Grandmother's driveway, humming under his breath.

"Okay, Keller, hang on," he said as he stepped on the accelerator. "This car doesn't have brakes and if I drive slower than sixty miles an hour, the engine dies."

"You're ridiculous," I told him. He was driving well within the speed limit.

"I know," he said. "But it keeps the boogeyman away."

I enjoyed the movie and the peach pie, but halfway through the pie I began worrying about what would happen next. Drew had been unusually silent, and several times during the movie, I was aware that he was watching me and not the screen. He didn't look at me often in the restaurant, but I had the feeling that he wanted to.

Was he going to take me directly home, or was he really planning a stop someplace behind the stadium or along a deserted road? I wasn't sure I wanted Drew to kiss me, and I didn't know how to get out of it.

But he drove me straight home and stopped the car close to Grandmother's porch, where the light still burned. I relaxed. He surely wouldn't kiss me when Grandmother could look out and see us clearly.

Drew studied me for a moment and then said soberly, "I sure like you."

Before I could say anything, he got out of the car, came around to my side and opened the door. "It's almost midnight," he said as he walked me to the porch. "I don't know what you turn into when the clock's through striking, but I'm a recovering neurotic and I can't stand any shocks. Good night, Keller."

He turned around, went back to the car, honked, and drove away. I wasn't sure whether or not I was supposed to laugh.

Grandmother was still up when I went in. "Did you have a good time?" she asked. She was in her bathrobe, rubbing lotion on her hands.

"It was a good movie. I liked it."

"And do you like Drew, too?"

"Sure. He's a nice guy. Peculiar but nice."

Grandmother put down her bottle of hand lotion. "That's true. I approve of him. Most of the time, that is."

I stared at her. "What does that mean?"

She smiled. "Oh, Keller, Drew can be an awful scamp. But who wants a fellow who's absolutely harmless?"

I shook my head, amazed at her. "Good night," I said. "I'd better go upstairs before you tell me things my parents don't want me to know."

I could hear her laughing as I closed my bedroom door. But I wasn't laughing. I was thinking about quiet, elusive Tom.

Was he harmless?

Nine

On Saturday morning, I wore jeans and a thick sweater because the sunlight held no heat. Autumn had come to Cascade. The wind blew bits of torn clouds from north to south across a bright sky. The leaves on the birch trees that lined the road were turning gold, and in the distance I could see the poplar trees by Tom's house flickering like candle flames.

Ripples on the pond glittered. The ducks had gone, flown south, I supposed. Lily pads, edged with yellow, partially concealed flashing darts of bright gold, Drew's fish. I had grown to love this peaceful place.

"Tom?" I called out. "Are you here?"

When he didn't answer, I dodged through the trees that stood between the pond and the house. Sunlight fell on the windows in an odd way, not creating polished reflections but instead turning the glass murky. Someone might have been watching me. I couldn't be certain.

"Tom?" I called. "Is that you?"

"Here I am," he shouted, behind me.

I turned and saw him and Troy coming out of the woods. My heart thudded. I was so happy I could have danced. He wore his white shirt again. Perhaps he had several, because I never saw him in anything else. He must be cold, I thought, suddenly concerned for him.

"I couldn't come yesterday because of the rain," I told him as he took my hand. I wanted to ask him if he missed me, but I didn't dare. What if he said that he'd been too busy and didn't notice that I hadn't shown up? What if he hadn't even been here?

He smiled at me, but his face looked drawn and weary, not happy. "I'm glad you're here," he said. "Let's go to the cliff. The trees are beautiful now. They're worth seeing."

"Aren't you cold?" I asked as we walked.

"No. I'm fine," he said. "How about you?"

"This is my heaviest sweater."

Troy leaped off the path then and ran under the trees. In the distance, I could hear something crashing around in the underbrush.

"He's pestering the deer," Tom said. "But he's careful not to get too close."

"They're probably not afraid of him."

"I hope they are," Tom said. "As long as they're afraid of all dogs, they won't trust the wrong one and end up hurt."

How terrible for the deer, I thought. I knew how it was to live like that. But I was taking risks now, and not just with Drew and Rose at school. Tom was the biggest risk I'd ever taken. If he rejected me, would I think that these afternoons with him had been worth it? The thought scared me.

"Are there still beavers in the pond?" I asked, to help myself through a bad moment. "I never see them."

Tom was quiet for a moment. "Sometimes I think I see them, but I can't be certain. I'd hate to think that they were all dead."

"Whatever happened to that boy who set the traps?"

"Elwood Bruce?" Tom's hand tightened on mine. "I don't know. If he ever comes here again —"

I squeezed his hand back. "Maybe he realizes what he did and he's sorry now."

"He's never sorry about anything," Tom said bitterly.

We'd reached the rocks on the edge of the cliff, and Troy was there waiting for us, panting and looking embarrassed.

"They got away again, didn't they?" Tom said, laughing.

We sat and leaned against the tall rock. Below us, the forest looked like an old tapestry, with splendid colors splayed against deep shadows.

But then the scene blurred and faded, and I thought that I saw houses there with the trees, shadows among the shadows. Streets lay in straight lines, intersecting. Glittering ghosts of cars traveled them.

I blinked and the houses and streets were gone.

"What's wrong?" Tom asked.

I rubbed my eyes impatiently. "I'm imagining things," I told him. "I thought I saw houses down there."

"There isn't a house between here and North Grange. That's why I like sitting here. Sometimes I think about what it must have been like before there were any people in this area, when there were only animals. And all the quiet." He closed his eyes and smiled.

Troy rested his chin on Tom's knees, sighed, and closed his eyes, too. The two of them seemed joined somehow, in a way that left me out.

"Tom, you've dropped out of school, haven't you?" I asked quietly, unable to help myself.

He opened his eyes, glanced at me, and then looked away. "I guess so." He didn't sound certain.

"You mean you have some sort of problem at school and you don't know where you stand?" Now that I'd started the questions I knew I shouldn't ask, I was desperate to grasp his situation completely.

"Not exactly," he said. He brushed his hand over his forehead. "I'll straighten it out."

"You look so tired," I blurted. "Are you sure you've been feeling all right?"

"I'm fine."

I waited until I was sure of my words. "Tom, the other day when I came here and I couldn't find you, I went up to the house. The kitchen curtains were gone. I didn't see them today, either. Have your parents gone away?"

He squeezed my hand again. "I think so."

I sat forward to look at him. "What do you mean you think so? I don't understand what's going on. Either they're gone or they aren't, Tom! Can't you tell me what's happened?"

82

He grabbed me and pulled me against him, hard, and didn't let go of me for a long time. He didn't say anything and I wanted to push away to see his face, to see if he was crying.

"Tom, please," I whispered. "I'll try to help you with whatever it is. But I don't know what to do if you don't tell me what's happened."

But still he didn't answer me.

What have I done? I asked myself. Something ugly has happened, and it's so bad that he's ashamed to tell me. Have his parents just deserted him, gone away and left him behind?

I could feel him breathing against my hair. But he didn't speak.

Perhaps his parents are dead, I thought. He doesn't have anyplace to go now, and he's embarrassed that no one wants him.

Or he's sick with something much worse than I have and he doesn't want me to know about it. He's run away from a hospital. He just made up a story about living here.

No. He made up the story because he's run away from some other town. He's done something terrible but it wasn't his fault, and now he can't go back.

"Tom," I whispered, "it's all right. You don't have to tell me anything."

"Will you come here again?" he asked.

"I'll always come back, until you tell me you don't want me here."

"Maybe you shouldn't come back anymore. But Keller, if you don't, I don't know what will happen to me."

We clung to each other until Troy began whining.

"What's wrong?" Tom asked him. "What's wrong, boy?"

Troy ran away from the cliff and back again, whimpering.

"I'd better go see what's bothering him," Tom said as he got to his feet. "I'll be back again as soon as I can."

He followed Troy into the woods. For a few minutes, I could hear them moving through the brush, but then the sounds stopped. I got to my feet.

"Tom?"

No answer. I took the path into the woods, calling Tom over and over, but he never answered me. I called Troy, too, but the dog didn't come to me.

Finally I went back to the pond and waited there for a long time. I didn't see Tom and his dog again, and I went home at last.

Late that afternoon I biked out to the pond once more. Tom wasn't there and he didn't answer me when I called. I didn't wait long that time.

But before I left, I went to the house and knocked on the door, even though I was certain that no one would come. My knocking echoed inside. I thought, for an instant, that a woman was sobbing in the house. But I was the one who wept.

"Is anybody there?" I cried. I remembered the traveler in de la Mare's poem, the loneliness.

If there were "listeners" in the house, they didn't answer.

Ten

I dreamed confused dreams of Tom that night, and in the morning all I could recall was uneasy, half recollections of rain and shadows, and Tom trying to tell me something that he didn't have words to say.

I didn't know how to help him. Telling anyone else in order to get help for him was out of the question until I knew what was going on. If my worst suspicion was right, that Tom had done something somewhere and was hiding at the old house, then I could betray him simply by trying to find help.

At breakfast, Grandmother asked me if I wanted to go to church. "Drew will be there, and quite a few other young people, too," she added.

"Maybe next week," I said as I poured juice in my glass.

Grandmother had invited me so many times that I wondered how she could resist asking me why I refused.

But all she ever said was, "Whenever you're ready."

I didn't go to church because church was too quiet. I only willingly went to public places if they were likely to be noisy. Even school was too quiet, although when necessary I could generate enough noise by scraping my feet and rustling papers to hide my asthma. Unless I was having a really bad attack, that is. I'd have needed to arrange a train wreck to cover that up.

Movies were sometimes too quiet, but I simply got up and went off to the bathroom where I could use my inhaler and wait until I felt better. But it was much harder to get up and walk out of church, especially if the minister was talking. Or during silent prayers. It's not that by that time everybody around me didn't know what was wrong. It's that I made everything worse by getting up and apologizing while I squeezed past whispering, staring people. So I stopped going to church while I was still in grade school. It was just one more thing I had learned to do without.

I didn't like knowing that people were whispering about me. And I hated being laughed at. I'd learned early that if you had a problem that some people thought was funny, they'd laugh no matter where you were. Just look at the savages who grin and poke each other when they see someone who's mentally retarded. Or when a stutterer tries to talk. Sometimes I wondered if people knew how cruel they were. Maybe they didn't, but I believed that they did. They were so eager to laugh.

Well, to be fair, there were some who didn't laugh. They were the ones who were embarrassed to be seen with me.

In any event, I couldn't have gone with Grandmother that morning. I had to get back to the pond.

There was a thick, wet fog outside, and Grandmother's car was out of sight while I could still hear it. I waited a few minutes, to make sure she wasn't going to come back for some reason, and then I took my bike out of the garage and rode toward the pond. I was afraid that Tom wouldn't be there but I went anyway, hoping I was wrong and that this would be the day I'd understand everything.

I couldn't find him. I even went to the cliff. Below me the fog hung over the forest, thicker there than it was anywhere else. I couldn't see the trees.

I went to the house, too, and knocked on the door again.

"Is someone home?" I asked. "My name is Keller Parrish and I'm looking for a boy named Tom Hurley. Can you hear me?"

No one answered. I walked away, head up, and I didn't cry until I reached the road.

By the time I got home, I was through crying. When Grandmother came in later, she didn't notice that my eyes were red.

"The Sennetts invited us for dinner," she said. "And Drew sends a message. He wants you to know that if you go, he'll take you to the video store and rent any tape you want to watch later on."

I didn't want to go there for dinner, but I could see that Grandmother did, so I agreed, pretending that I was glad. I even dressed up for the occasion. That really pleased her.

87

It pleased Drew, too. When we got to his house, he circled around me twice, grinning, and said finally, "She looks pretty good, doesn't she? We'll let her stay."

His mother, who looked like Drew and even wore glasses, came up behind him and gave him a light shove. "Hello, Keller, I've heard lots about you and most of it was reasonably rational." She thrust out her hand and I shook it. I liked her.

Drew's father wandered in, holding a thick book and seeming slightly absent-minded. "Beth?" he said to Grandmother. "You here already?"

"It's almost time to eat," Mrs. Sennett said briskly. "Here's Keller, Beth's granddaughter."

I shook hands with him, too. He smiled shyly at me. "Are you the new girl at school?"

"No, she's an old girl that they let hang around the halls to give the school atmosphere," Drew said. "Come on, Keller. I'll show you my collection of naughty postcards up in my bedroom."

"Drew," his mother said, her voice heavy with warning. "Take Keller in and introduce her to your grandmother."

Drew led me into the living room where an attractive older woman was playing a video game with a little boy. Drew introduced her as Granny, and she made a face at him.

"I'm Eloise Sennett," she said to me. "I was invited here today especially to meet you. Please forgive me for not greeting you at the door, but I'm beating young Barry here at this perfectly disgusting game and I didn't want to take a chance that he'd get ahead of me if I turned my back on him.'' She ruffled the boy's dark hair and he grinned, but he didn't take his eyes off the television screen.

"My brother is eight, but he's not working out so we're getting rid of him before he gets any older," Drew said.

"Don't you wish," Barry scoffed cheerfully without looking up.

The screen exploded with colored lights, bells rang, and Mrs. Sennett burst out laughing. "I actually won," she said. "I can't believe it. This little thief beats everybody."

Barry looked at me. "You wanna play now?"

I shook my head. "I always lose at those games, so I gave up."

Drew took my hand. "I wasn't going to let you play. Remember the postcards up in my room."

"Oh, Drew, for heaven's sake," his grandmother said. "Leave her alone." She patted the couch next to where she sat. "Come here, Keller, and tell me why you waste your time on this clown."

Drew sat down on the floor at her feet and looked at me. He obviously expected me to answer, even if she didn't.

"He makes me laugh," I said.

"Well, at least you didn't gross me out and say you liked him," Barry said, and he giggled, waiting for Drew's reaction.

"It wouldn't have grossed *me* out," Drew said calmly.

His mother called us for dinner then, and we took our places at a long table in the dining room. Drew sat next to me, and as soon as he took his place he nudged my foot with his.

"I meant what I said," he whispered.

I picked up my napkin and avoided his gaze. He was weird and funny and liked me too much. Sooner or later I'd have to deal with that.

During dessert, Mr. Sennett said something about the Hurley house that I didn't hear. I looked up sharply.

"Keller rides her bike down the road as far as Deerfield Pond," Grandmother said.

"What about it?" I asked, wishing I'd been listening.

"The old house is going to be torn down," Mr. Sennett said. "The new owners are putting up a big house and a barn for their horses."

I knew Drew was staring at me, but I didn't care. "What about the Hurleys?" I asked.

"Oh, the place has been vacant for years," Mr. Sennett said.

"How long?" I asked. Everyone was staring at me then.

Drew's grandmother answered. "The Hurleys left more than thirty years ago."

The Hurleys who moved out that long ago might have been Tom's grandparents, I thought. "No one ever came back? Not even their children?"

"They didn't have any children," Drew's grandmother said. "Well, there'd been one who died years before they moved. Mr. Hurley's cousin inherited the place, and he sold it a few months ago."

I picked up my water glass and took a big swallow. Tom must be related to the cousin, I thought. His son or grandson. And he's been staying there because he can't stay anywhere else. Does he know the house is going to be torn down? What will he do then?

"Keller's going to like the horses," Grandmother said. "Riding down to see them should be a lot more fun than looking at an abandoned house."

Drew saw me glance at him and he shrugged. I was sure he was remembering that I'd asked about Tom. What was he thinking? Was he going to say anything?

When dinner was over at last, Drew asked me if I wanted to go with him and Barry while they rented a tape. I didn't. I wanted to go home, get my bike, and ride down the road again. Tom had to know that the house was going to be torn down so that he could make other plans for himself.

But Grandmother clearly had no intention of leaving yet, and Barry was clamoring to go to the video store. Drew, watching me closely, didn't smile when I finally agreed to go.

When we got outside, he said, "Do you want to make a detour before we go get the tape?"

"What do you mean?" I asked.

"Would you like to go for a little ride out Birch Road, for instance?

"What for?" I asked defiantly, holding my chin up. I didn't want him asking questions about Tom, or looking for him, either.

He lifted his shoulders helplessly. "You looked so upset at the table. I thought maybe you'd want to get out there and tell your friend that he's going to have to leave."

"Why didn't you tell me that you knew that house was going to be torn down?"

"I didn't know until Dad said so at dinner. That guy you asked me about, Tom Hurley, he lives out there alone, doesn't he?"

"I guess."

"What's he done? Run away?"

"I don't know. Just never mind, okay?"

Barry, who'd been getting his jacket from his room, rushed at us, shouting, "Let's go before all the good tapes are gone."

"Is that okay, Keller? First stop at the store?" Drew asked.

"First and only stop," I said. "And just forget that I ever asked you if you knew Tom."

But Drew didn't promise.

I couldn't concentrate on anything. At the store, Barry chose the tape but I couldn't remember the name of it by the time we got in the car.

"Why are you breathing so funny?" Barry asked me on the way back.

"Sit down and fasten your seat belt," Drew shouted crossly.

"But I only wanted to know —" Barry cried.

"Nobody can breathe when you're in the car," Drew said. "You smell like stale bubble gum and peanut butter."

"I do not!" Barry shouted.

"If you don't sit down and fasten your belt, I'm going to take the tape back to the store," Drew said.

Barry sat down and was silent for the rest of the ride.

As soon as we got to the Sennetts', I went straight to the bathroom and used my inhaler. In the mirror over the basin, I saw how pale I was. I rubbed my cheeks hard, to make them pink before I went back out.

While we were watching the movie, I kept looking at my watch, wishing Grandmother would get tired and want to go home. But it was dark before she suggested it, too late for me to go to the pond.

Drew walked out to the car with us. While Grandmother was settling herself behind the wheel, Drew bent close to me. "I'll see you tomorrow, okay?"

"Sure," I said, surprised.

He looked at me too long. "I believe you," he said.

Before I could say anything, he closed the car door, rapped twice on the top, and ran for his porch.

"Are you feeling all right?" Grandmother asked as soon as she started the car.

"Of course," I said.

"You don't look it. And you've been having trouble breathing. I could tell."

That was what Drew meant, then. He was wondering if I was sick again and probably staying home from school the next day.

For a crazy moment, I'd wondered if he thought I was going to leave Cascade with Tom.

Eleven

On Monday, I spent most of my school hours looking out windows. The sky was overcast and sullen, but there was no rain. Tom was on my mind. I had to warn him that the house was going to be torn down soon.

Grandmother wasn't home when I got there after school. I didn't waste time congratulating myself on my luck, but threw down my books and ran for my bike.

High above me, half a dozen crows played dangerous games in the wind, shrieking and diving at each other. When they noticed me speeding down the road, they followed. They gave me shivers. I'd always been half-afraid of crows.

When I reached the driveway to the Hurley house, I let my bike fall to the ground and raced toward the woods, shouting Tom's name.

I heard Troy first, barking in the distance. Then Tom

came out of the woods, slowly. He stopped when he saw me.

I hurried to him, anxious to tell him what I'd learned at the Sennetts'. He listened to me, his head bent a little, and when I was done, he took my hand.

"It's all right," he said. "Don't be afraid. It's going to be all right."

I gripped his hand hard. "Tom, you have to leave here! Don't you understand? It won't be safe for you here anymore."

"Don't worry. Please. Come with me and we'll walk for a while."

We followed the path through the woods, holding hands. "What will you do?" I asked him. "Where will you go?"

"I don't know yet." He sounded so tired that he frightened me.

"Are you all right?" I asked. I was shaking. "Tom, you're scaring me."

He didn't say anything. He held a branch out of my way and snapped his fingers for Troy, who was falling behind, head down, tail drooping.

"You're sick, aren't you? You don't even have a jacket, and the nights are cold now. Is there a blanket in the house? What do you do for food?"

"Hush, Keller," he said gently. "Let's not spend our time together looking for things to worry about. Sit down on the rock. We'll warm up when we're out of the wind."

I leaned against Tom, and Troy crouched against his legs. The wind moaned around us, but we were sheltered by the tall rock behind us. Heavy clouds streamed overhead.

"I love storms," Tom said. "I love the sound and the feel of the wind, and the way the air smells."

His face was pale but he was smiling as he looked up at the sky. How could he be so calm? It was all I could do to keep from crying.

"You have to tell me what you're going to do," I said. "I can't stand not knowing if I'll ever see you again." As I spoke, I was coming to a slow understanding of myself. "Tom, I don't get sick when I'm with you. Not even now, when I'm upset. What would I do without you?"

"I can't take credit because you feel better. Somehow you did that for yourself. But I'm glad, though."

"Say that I'll see you again," I begged. Tears ran down my face.

He bent his head and kissed me gently once, twice. "Oh, Keller, don't you know that things don't always turn out the way we want them to?"

"We can talk to my grandmother," I suggested eagerly, desperately. "If I told her how you saved me, she'd want to help you." Even while I said it, I knew that my suggestion was irrational. Grandmother might be grateful that Tom had kept me from drowning, but I couldn't imagine her involving herself with someone who would not, or could not, even explain his problem.

But Tom said, "No."

I closed my eyes for a moment and took a deep breath. "It's that bad, then? The trouble you're in?"

His hand closed down hard on my shoulder, "I'm not sure."

"Can't you tell me what it is?"

He hesitated, then shook his head.

"If you're worried that Grandmother might turn you in, then we won't tell her. I'll find another place for you to stay and get you the things you need."

He was so quiet that I didn't know what to expect. He was looking out over the valley, but his gold-flecked eyes were focused on something I couldn't see.

"Tom? You'll let me help you, won't you?"

He put his arm around me and leaned his cheek against my hair. "I'll try," he said. I didn't understand his answer.

Rain spattered down and we got to our feet. "You have to go," Tom said. "Hurry."

I hurried, but not for myself. Tom would take shelter in the house if I was gone, I thought. He kissed me good-bye and I saw him watching me as I rode away.

I got home just as the rain began falling in blinding sheets. When Grandmother walked in half an hour later, I'd changed clothes and was busy in the kitchen making a salad for dinner.

"Isn't this rain awful?" she asked as she pulled off her coat. "I hope we're not going to have an early winter."

"Maybe not." I said. I looked at the window, where rain gushed down the glass. "September weather is really strange. Remember last year? It got so hot in Seattle at the end of the month that people started watering their lawns all over again."

"That's too much to hope for, two years in a row," Grandmother said. She was setting the table quickly and nervously. "You look sad, Keller. What's wrong?"

"When bad weather comes, I worry about all the stray dogs and cats in the world." Tom and his dog. They were strays and winter was coming. I looked down and blinked hard.

The next day, Miss Penny gave me an A for my sketch of Tom and asked me if I'd exhibit it in the school art show in the spring. "You can leave it here until then," she said. "I'll keep it in the cupboard and help you mount it before the show."

"I'd rather take it home." I didn't want to think of the sketch put away on a dark shelf in the cupboard for months. It belonged with me. "I'll bring it back," I told her.

She looked at me a little strangely but let me take the sketch with me when I left class.

Rose helped me roll up the sketch so it would fit in my locker. I wondered how I was going to manage it on the bus after school. If it was damaged or even badly wrinkled, I knew I'd never be able to do another one that looked so much like Tom.

Drew sauntered up then. "What are the two of you doing? Is that wallpaper for your locker, Keller? Would you like a folding cot and a camp stove? I can probably find you a lamp and a coffee table in our attic."

"It's a sketch," Rose said. "Why don't you offer her a ride home so she doesn't have to take it on the bus?"

"Sure." Drew looked curiously at the roll of paper. "What did you draw?"

"Me, of course," Rose lied.

Drew lost interest. "I'll pick you up in front of the building after our last class," he said to me.

After he left, I said. "You didn't have to lie to him, Rose. Now I feel guilty."

She suddenly looked sad. "I didn't do it for you, I did it for Drew. He's crazy about you. If he saw the sketch you drew of Tom, he'd feel bad even if he pretended he didn't care."

"It's only a sketch," I said.

"Of a guy who's so romantic-looking he makes my teeth ache," Rose said. "Any boy would be jealous, Keller. Wake up. I wish you'd just get it over with and tell Drew that you're definitely going with somebody else. Then he wouldn't always be hoping."

"You're exaggerating how he feels," I told her. "He's not that serious."

But he was and I knew it.

Drew picked me up at the main entrance after school and didn't say a word about the sketch until he stopped the car in Grandmother's driveway. Then, without even asking, he took it off the back seat where'd I'd put it and unrolled it carefully.

Neither of us said anything for a long time.

Drew sighed and rolled the sketch back up. "I guess that's the bottom line, then," he said.

"I don't know what you mean," I said. But I did.

"It's the guy you think lives out at Deerfield Pond."

"Yes."

"The one who calls himself Tom Hurley?"

I nodded.

Drew frowned. "I have an awful feeling that you're involved with someone who's in some sort of trouble. Does your grandmother know about him?"

"No."

"Why not? If he's okay, why hasn't he been around so she can meet him?"

I couldn't answer him.

He sighed again. "That's what I was afraid of. What kind of trouble is he in?"

"I don't know," I said. "But it's not anything awful. I'm sure of it." I hoped I sounded convincing.

Drew poked at his glasses. "What's he going to do when the house is torn down?"

"He doesn't know yet."

"Are you sure of what you're doing, Keller?"

"Yes," I said. "No. I don't know. I just know that I'd be dead if it hadn't been for Tom. He saved my life. I was drowning in that pond. I couldn't breathe. He pulled me out."

"Jeez," Drew said. "Now you think you owe your life to him?"

"It's not like that! He's nice. He cares about the animals that live out there. Did you know that someone put beaver traps in the pond? His dog got caught in one and nearly died."

Drew stared at me. "There aren't any beavers in that pond. I've been out there hundreds of times and I never saw a beaver."

"I saw the dog's hurt foot," I declared. "I know it's true."

"What creep set the trap?"

"A boy named Elwood Bruce," I said. "Do you know him?"

Drew shook his head. "There's nobody at school named Elwood Bruce. The only Bruce I know is an old guy and I don't know his first name. He lives alone and he drinks too much. I can't see him managing to set traps anywhere."

"Well, there's an Elwood Bruce somewhere and he nearly killed Tom's dog!" I cried.

Drew's mouth tightened. "Take it easy. I wasn't calling you a liar."

"But you're calling Tom a liar."

"Not that either. I just can't figure out what's going on."

"All right, then come out to the pond with me. I'll introduce you to Tom. And his dog. Then you'll see."

I'd blurted it out before I realized what I'd done. I grabbed Drew's arm. "Promise you won't tell anybody they're out there."

Drew looked straight at me. "I won't. Look, go in and tell your grandmother that we're going for a ride."

"Are we going to the pond?"

Drew nodded. "I'm going to hate myself tomorrow, but maybe there's something I can do. I'll listen to what the guy has to say for himself, anyway."

I rushed in the house, told Grandmother that Drew and I were going for a ride, and ran back out before she had a chance to object.

As I got in beside him, Drew looked at me soberly.

"I won't let anything bad happen to you." He started the car.

"Nothing bad's going to happen to me," I told him. "But I'm afraid for Tom."

Drew didn't say anything. When we got to the Hurley place, he parked the car in the driveway close to the house and turned in his seat to face me. "Okay, where is this guy? In the house?"

"He's usually over by the pond or in the woods," I said as I opened the car door. "Come on. I'll call him."

I hurried ahead of Drew. Tom wasn't at the pond, so I called him several times, expecting him to come out of the woods then.

Drew waited, hands in his pockets, looking down into the water where his goldfish swam under drifting willow leaves.

I started toward the path that led through the woods, but I stopped uncertainly. Perhaps Tom wouldn't come out because he'd seen Drew. If I led Drew to the cliff, Tom might feel he had to hide. I wasn't being fair to him.

"I guess he's not around," I said. I walked over by Drew and looked down in the water, feeling foolish.

"Maybe he doesn't want to meet me," Drew said.

He was probably right. My eyes filled with tears.

"Come on, let's go," Drew said. "I shouldn't have brought you out here."

I looked at the woods once more and drew in a sharp breath. There Tom stood, in the shadows, with Troy beside him.

"There he is!" I cried. "Tom! It's all right, Tom!"

I started for him, but Drew grabbed my arm. "I don't see anybody," he said. "Don't go off into the woods, Keller."

I pointed at Tom. "He's there. See, under the trees? He's looking straight at us."

But even as I spoke, Tom withdrew deeper into the shadows. Troy lingered, though, watching us.

"It's only a dog," Drew said.

"Tom!" I shouted.

But Tom didn't come back. Troy ran after him and vanished.

I burst into tears of frustration. "I can't believe I did this!" I cried. "He thinks I've betrayed him. He'll run away now and I'll never see him again."

Drew watched the woods and didn't answer for a moment. "You've seen that dog before? Is that the one who was caught in the trap?"

"Yes. His name is Troy."

Drew nodded slowly. "I don't think there's anything we can do here now. I'll take you home, Keller. Maybe we can come back some other time."

"Sure," I said, but I swore to myself that I'd never bring Drew or anybody else to the pond again.

He took me home and walked to the door with me. He didn't speak.

"Do you want to come in?" I asked reluctantly.

"No, thanks," Drew said. He sounded cool and distant. "I'll see you at school tomorrow."

I was embarrassed, but before I could say anything,

he ran down the steps and climbed in his car. I watched him leave, dismayed that he hadn't honked the way he always had before.

He thinks I'm ridiculous, I told myself as I went inside. He thinks I have a crush on a tramp who's living in a vacant house.

I went upstairs to my room and pinned the sketch to the inside of my closet door, where Grandmother was not likely to see it. For a long time I looked at it. My chest hurt. I was having trouble breathing. I couldn't stop crying.

When Grandmother came up to call me for dinner, my closet door was closed and I was hanging onto my window sill, trying to gulp in fresh air.

"Oh, my God," Grandmother said. "I'll get the car."

Twelve

I didn't wake up until ten o'clock the next day because the doctor in the emergency room the night before had given me a strong sedative to take when I got home. When my eyes opened, I lay very still for a moment, intensely aware of my lungs. They were sore. The muscles in my back hurt. But I could breathe freely when I climbed out of bed.

Outside my window, the world looked as calm as I felt. I was detached, an observer of my own life. I always felt that way after I'd been desperately sick, probably because of the medication I'd been given. At those times I could convince myself that I'd never be that sick again, that I'd gone through the worst that could ever happen. I never remembered until later how many times I'd felt that way before, or how often I'd been disappointed. Maybe I didn't want to remember.

Once I was in the hospital with a girl who had nearly

died from eating something that had caused a violent allergic reaction. Melanie had suffered from anaphylactic shock, stopped breathing, and lost consciousness. In our hospital room we became good friends, and we agreed to get together, after we were discharged, for lunch and a visit to the Science Fair at Seattle Center. I thought that at last I'd have a friend who knew what I went through because she went through it, too — and even worse.

We met for lunch a few weeks later, and she asked the waitress if anything had been cooked in peanut oil, which was what made her ill. The waitress was rude and impatient, but she went to ask the cook and came back a minute later to say that the cook didn't use peanut oil. But halfway through the meal, Melanie stopped eating and said, "Help me." Her face was gray and sweat broke out on her forehead.

I didn't know what to do. "Do you have an inhaler?" I asked.

She gestured toward her purse and I opened it. Inside was a long, thin plastic box. Melanie grabbed for it, missed, and stood up, hands pressed to her chest. Her lips were blue.

I opened the box and saw a hypodermic needle inside. "Is this what you want?" I asked Melanie.

She fell to the floor, knocking over her chair.

I'd never given an injection and I didn't know what to do. During the first seconds, the women at the next table only stared, but then one of them stood up, a little uncertainly, and said, "Has she fainted?"

"She can't breathe," I said and I knelt by Melanie.

"Call Medic One," the woman said to one of her friends. "Now."

I should have thought of that. Medic One is Seattle's lightning fast medical emergency service and everybody there knows about it. But my mind was blank. The woman pushed me away and bent over Melanie, her ear at Melanie's mouth.

"See? She's not breathing!" I cried.

"Did she choke on something?"

"No! She's allergic!" I thrust the case containing the needle at the woman. "Give her a shot!"

The woman hesitated, studying the needle, blinking hard. "I'm afraid," she whispered. Seconds ticked by while she read the instructions printed inside the box.

"She'll die if you don't give her the shot," I babbled.

Someone shouted, "Medic One's coming!" and I heard a siren in the distance.

I couldn't bear what was happening. Melanie was dying right in front of us. I bit my lip until it bled, and when the Medics ran in, I was crying.

They saved her. But afterward Melanie had a stroke while she was in the hospital. Occasionally we'd talk on the phone, but I had trouble understanding her. I always thought about her when I was recovering.

So I thought about her again, while I was looking out my window in Grandmother's house. What would Melanie have to say about Tom? Maybe I'd write her a letter and tell her about him.

Grandmother knocked on my door and came in. "I thought I heard you get up. How are you this morning?"

I turned away from the window. "I'm just tired."

"You look a little shaky," Grandmother said. "Get back in bed and I'll bring you something to eat."

"I'm not hungry." I was never hungry afterward.

"I'll bring you something anyway," she said. "You're even thinner than you were when you came. Your parents are going to be furious with me. They thought I'd be able to take care of you better than this."

"I don't need taking care of, honestly," I told her. She looked as if she was ready to cry. "I'm really pretty strong. Isn't that what Mom said when you called her last night?"

Grandmother grinned crookedly. "How did you know?"

"She said the same thing last time."

"It doesn't make me feel any better," Grandmother said.

"Remember, they've been through this lots of times. Afterward I feel fine. It's just like the doctor says — panic makes everything worse." It was easy for me to talk like that while I was still affected by the medication. In another day I'd be back wondering why I had to be stuck with something as rotten and embarrassing as asthma.

"I get more scared than you do, I suppose," Grandmother said.

I laughed a little. "I doubt that." I got back in bed and pulled the blankets over me. She may have brought me breakfast, but I fell asleep and didn't wake up again until late that afternoon.

In the evening I dressed and went downstairs for dinner. My parents called while we were eating dessert, first to reassure themselves that I was feeling better and then to give me some news.

"We're coming to Cascade Friday afternoon," Mom said.

"We're going to look at a house," Dad said from the extension phone. They always talked to me at the same time.

"Then you might move here sooner than you thought?" I asked.

"Well, maybe," Mom said doubtfully. "Even if the house in Cascade turns out to be something we'd like, we still have to sell the house in Seattle."

"I could send your mother on to Cascade and stay here myself until our house is sold," Dad said.

"I'd crowd Beth too much," Mom said to him. "We should leave the house vacant." As usual, they were having their own conversation between the kitchen and living room.

I started laughing. "Why don't you two hang up and settle this? I'll see you Friday and you can tell me what you've decided."

"Put the coffee on, Jack," Mom said to Dad.

I said good-bye and hung up. Grandmother was watching me, curious about the conversation.

When I told her, she said, "I told them about the house Mrs. Ashburn showed us the day we picked up your bike. They must have contacted the owner."

I didn't remember much about the house, except that it was far away from Deerfield Pond. But that wasn't going to matter much longer, because Tom had to find another place to stay.

I was too tired that evening to ride my bike. But Tom was on my mind. I was ashamed that I'd slept away most of the day instead of trying to think up a solution to his problems.

Tomorrow we'll talk again, I promised myself. There has to be an answer.

Drew called me later, as I was starting upstairs to go to bed.

"Did I miss anything at school?" I asked after I answered all the standard questions about my health.

"Nothing important," he said.

"Okay, then," I told him. "I'm tired so I think I'll go back to bed."

"Don't hang up!" he said urgently. "I've got something interesting to show you."

"Hold it up to the phone," I said, laughing.

"This is serious. I did some library research this afternoon. Appreciate me, because I haven't even had dinner yet."

"I don't know what I'm supposed to appreciate you for until you tell me what you're talking about. What were you doing at the library? Driving your grandmother crazy again?"

"Listen, no more funny business. I've got to show you something right away. Do you think you can go for a short ride with me?"

"I know Grandmother won't let me," I said. "You'll have to tell me about it."

I waited, listening to him breathe faintly. "You won't believe me," he said. "You've got to read it for yourself. Look, how about sneaking out later? I'll stop up the road a little way and you can read this stuff with a flashlight.''

"What stuff?" I demanded.

"It's about Tom Hurley."

My hand tightened on the phone. "What about him?"

"Meet me when you think it's safe. Eleven? Midnight? I'll wait around the corner. Name the time.''

I bit my lip. Grandmother went to bed at eleven. She'd be asleep by twelve. "Twelve," I whispered.

"I think you're going to be really interested in this. Jeez, I hope I'm doing the right thing.'' His last words were muttered, almost to himself.

"I don't know what you're talking about," I said.

"You will. I'll see you at midnight. Bye.''

When I hung up, Grandmother called out, asking if that was Drew.

"Yes. He was worried.''

"Did you miss something important at school? You sounded a little upset.''

I started up the stairs, not wanting her to come out of the living room for fear she could read my face. "Oh, you know Drew. He can't tell a story without exaggerating it so much that you don't know what's true and what isn't.'' I pretended to laugh.

Once in my room, I leaned against my door for a moment. I could see myself in my mirror. My face was pale, my eyes ringed with smudges. What did Drew know about Tom that couldn't wait until school tomorrow?

I turned out my light and waited. After I heard

Grandmother come upstairs to bed, I dressed quietly and waited some more. My bedside clock read 11:35 when I heard her open her window a crack, the last thing she did before getting into bed. Would she fall asleep right away? Sometimes she didn't.

I watched out my window. My eyes had become accustomed to the dark, and I saw a car turn at the corner and disappear behind a row of poplar trees. My clock said 11:50. Still I waited.

At two minutes before midnight, I eased my door open and closed it behind me. My heart hammered so loudly that I was sure Grandmother, at the other end of the hall, could hear it. I crept down the stairs and out the front door, grateful that I wasn't wheezing. But just in case, I felt my pocket again, to be sure I had my inhaler.

The night air was damp and cold, a combination that often made me ill. But my excitement had reached such a pitch that I was full of adrenaline. Later, I'd pay for it. But later I'd know what Drew had found out about Tom.

Drew turned on his headlights when he saw me coming, and I ran around to the passenger side of his car. As soon as I was inside, he started the engine.

"We'll go about a mile down the road," he said. "No one drives down that far."

"Be sure you don't go any farther. I wouldn't want Tom to see us and wonder what's going on."

Drew didn't respond, but I felt an odd chill that didn't have anything to do with the temperature inside the car. Drew doesn't like Tom, I thought. He's found out what

Tom did. Maybe it's something awful. But there'll be an explanation for it! Tom's too nice to have done something terrible.

I was wringing my hands by the time Drew stopped the car. He reached across me and took a flashlight and an envelope from the glove compartment.

"Hold this," he said, handing me the flashlight. "Now switch it on."

I directed the light to the envelope as he opened it and took out several pieces of paper. They looked like photocopies of newspaper articles.

"Here's the first one," he said. He held it up for me to read but his hand was shaking.

"What's wrong with you?" I asked as I took the paper from him. "Are you cold?"

"No. Read that."

The headline of the article read, "Tragedy at Deerfield Pond." Under that, I saw a photo and I bent close to the paper. "It looks like Tom," I said hoarsely. My eyes blurred. Tragedy! What could have happened?

"Read the date," Drew told me.

" 'September eleventh, nineteen forty-six.' "

"Now read the article."

" 'Yesterday morning Thomas Hurley, seventeen, drowned in the pond of his father's Cascade farm when he attempted to rescue the family dog, which had been caught underwater in a beaver trap. The trap chain tangled around the boy's leg, preventing him from reaching the surface.' "

I couldn't read any more. "That's terrible," I said. 'Do you suppose that this was one of Tom's relatives?

Maybe Tom was named after him." I peered at the picture again. "They look alike."

Drew handed me another sheet of paper. It was the obituary for the boy who had drowned in 1946. I pushed it away.

He handed me still another page. The headline read, "Police Search for Trapper." The article told of the efforts the county police were making to find the person who set the illegal trap on private property, causing the boy to drown.

I folded the pages together and handed them back to Drew. I was sick with relief. He didn't know anything about Tom, my Tom.

Drew took the flashlight from me and turned it off.

"Well?" I prompted.

"Keller, wake up," he said quietly.

"Wake up to what?" I demanded. "You bring me out here to show me some copies of old newspaper articles and I don't know what you want me to do with them. I don't even know where you got them."

"From the library basement. The Cascade *Bulletin* closed down fifteen years ago, but Granny saved a copy of every issue. I asked her what she knew about the Hurley family and she remembered a little about a boy who drowned more than forty years ago. It took me three hours to find the right papers."

"It's a sad story. And what's even worse, the same thing nearly happened all over again to another Tom Hurley."

"Keller," Drew said, "there was no other Tom Hurley."

"Maybe there are Hurley cousins who are teenagers now," I said bewilderedly.

"No. Granny says the youngest one is in his forties."

"Are you telling me that Tom lied to me? That he isn't Tom Hurley and his dog didn't nearly drown in the pond?"

Drew cleared his throat. "Granny remembered the reason Tom's family moved away about ten years later. They kept seeing him out by the pond and they couldn't take it anymore. They wouldn't sell the place, either, because they didn't want strangers there."

"What are you talking about?" I shouted. "That's the dumbest story I ever heard."

"But," Drew went on doggedly, "after Tom's parents died, their cousin went ahead and sold it because he never believed the story about Tom's ghost being at the pond."

"Shut up!" I raised my fists and then dropped them in my lap. "How dare you say that!" I said. "You're calling me crazy. I know Tom Hurley! He's real. He's not some imaginary boy his parents invented because they felt so bad. I even kissed him!"

Drew averted his head quickly, as if I'd slapped him.

"You made this up because you're jealous!" I raged. "I know you like me, but you know that I love Tom and this is what you're doing to get even. I'm surprised you didn't call the police and tell them he's hiding there. Is that what you'll do next?"

"Keller," Drew said, and his voice broke, "either the guy out there is a liar with something to hide or there's no one living at the pond. Everybody around here believes that the house is empty and it's been that way since before you were born. You either fell in love with a liar or he's the Tom who died in nineteen forty-six. And I think that you know which he is.''

''Take me to the pond and I'll prove that Tom's alive and he's not a liar!'' I cried. ''Right now! I'll go to the house and get Tom. Or if he's not there, I'll find him in the woods. You'll see!''

Drew just sat there.

''Start the car! I'm going to show you that you're wrong!''

Drew started the car. He didn't speak to me again while we drove to the old Hurley house. I leaped out of the car before he'd come to a complete stop and I ran up on the porch.

''Tom!'' I screamed, banging on the door with both my fists. ''Come out! I need to talk to you!''

I didn't care if I woke half the county. I didn't care about anything. The things Drew said couldn't be true.

No one came to the door. My shouts echoed in the quiet night. After a while, when I'd stopped crying, Drew came and led me away. He didn't say anything.

On the way home, I said, ''Tom is not a liar. And I don't believe in ghosts. You may, but then I think you're crazy anyway. But I'm not. I've never believed in stuff like that and I'm not going to start now.''

I was having a hard time breathing. I took out my inhaler and defiantly used it. I didn't care what Drew thought now.

He didn't respond to anything I said. When he got

about half a block from my house, he stopped to let me out.

"I hope you'll do me one favor," I said coldly as I opened the door. "Don't blab this all over school. I know I can't stop you, but if you do, I'll just quit going to classes. No one can make me go if I don't want to. And I'm not going to if you've made a fool out of me in front of everybody."

"I won't tell anyone," Drew said softly.

I shut the car door and walked off, not looking back. Grandmother didn't hear me return, even though I didn't try very hard to be quiet. I went to bed and lay awake most of the night hating Drew. I didn't want to know about the drowning that happened so long ago, and he must have suspected that. But he forced the information on me anyway.

That whole idea about the ghost was ridiculous. Stupid. Tom was real, and he wasn't a liar, either.

Drew was the liar.

Thirteen

I planned to go to school Thursday morning, even though I was tired and often needed to use my inhaler. I dressed carefully in my favorite sweater and skirt and spent extra time on my hair with the hope that Grandmother wouldn't notice how pale I was. All through breakfast, I chattered mindlessly, doing my best to make her laugh.

"Tomorrow," I told her, "when Mom and Dad get here, we'll all go look at that house and if it suits us, we have this one moved next door. I don't want to be that far away from your pancakes."

"I'm glad to see your appetite pick up like this." She slid two more pancakes on my plate and I ate them, even though I had a hard time swallowing. She was smiling when I left the house.

I got through the school day by will power. Between classes I ducked into a stall in the girls' john and flushed the water so that no one could hear the hissing sound my inhaler made. I was using it too much, so my heart pounded against my ribs, but I couldn't take a chance on having to leave school early because I was sick again. I wanted to go to the pond after school, and if Grandmother even suspected that I didn't feel well, she'd refuse to let me out of the house.

I spent my lunchtime in the library, looking at magazines. Rose believed me when I said I ate too big a breakfast to want lunch, too. She had no reason to suspect that I was avoiding Drew.

I wouldn't look at him. He didn't try to talk to me, which was a good thing, because I didn't want to be put in the position of asking him to let me alone. But I would have, if he'd forced the issue. I worried that he might have told people about Tom and me, but no one said anything or teased me. In fact, no one paid any attention to me at all.

Rose wanted to get together after school, but I told her that Grandmother expected me to rest, since I'd been sick the day before.

She touched my arm sympathetically. "I'm sorry. It must be hard."

"I'm used to it," I said. Instead of wanting to run away from her uncomplicated compassion, I found myself simply accepting it and being grateful that she cared. But would she understand about Tom? I didn't trust our tentative friendship enough to test it.

After school, I changed into jeans and a sweatshirt and wheeled my bike out of the garage even before I told Grandmother that I was going riding.

"Are you sure that's a good idea?" she asked uncertainly.

"The doctor in Seattle told me that the quicker I went back to exercising, the better off I'd be," I said truthfully.

Grandmother shook her head. "Don't stay out too long, then. The sky is clear now, but it can cloud up fast this time of year."

I opened the door. "I'll be back long before dinner."

Free. I pedaled fast until I knew I was out of sight, and then I slowed down and used my inhaler with one hand. Fortunately the road was level most of the way and the afternoon was windless and still.

I left my bike in Tom's driveway. I couldn't see him, and I didn't want to go to the house and knock after the way I'd behaved the night before. What if he'd heard me and didn't feel like talking to anybody who would make a scene like that?

Casually I started across the field, as if I didn't care whether he was there or not. But I watched out of the corner of my eye to see if he came out of the woods. When he did, I realized suddenly that I'd been afraid he wouldn't, afraid that he was really a ghost, a product of my imagination or the result of all the medicine I took.

I waved and restrained myself from running toward him. His smile was so joyous that I told myself that he hadn't heard my disgraceful racket the night before. He held out his hand and I took it.

"It's about time," he said. "I was afraid you wouldn't come today."

"I come whenever I can."

"I waited and waited for you yesterday," he said. He brushed one hand over his forehead. "Yes, it was yesterday."

"I had an appointment in North Grange," I said. "But I'm here now." I looked around. "Where's Troy?"

"He's sleeping on the rock by the cliff. I don't think he's feeling very well. He seems so tired."

"Is his foot infected?" I asked.

Tom shook his head. "Come with me and look at him. He acts as if he's worn out. He never chases after anything anymore, and sometimes I can't find him. I call him but he doesn't come."

The trees in the woods dropped leaves silently as we walked. Quail, startled by our passage, took flight and scolded us from low branches. I heard something run through the brush in the distance, but I wasn't afraid. I was growing accustomed to the sounds here.

We found Troy lying on the rock ledge, the late afternoon sun shining on him. His fur looked lifeless and dull, and when I touched him, his eyes opened only for a moment before he slept again. The tags on his collar seemed tarnished.

I lifted the foot that had been injured by the trap and examined it, but I couldn't see the place where the trap jaws had cut him. "It's completely healed," I said.

"I know."

"It looks as if nothing had ever really happened," I said slowly, not wanting to think what I was thinking, that Troy could never have been caught by a trap again, because he'd been dead for a long time. Drew. Damn him for telling me something so terrible that I couldn't bring myself to repeat it even as a joke.

Tom and I sat down next to each other, and he kept one hand on Troy, fondling his ears gently. The forest stretched out like a dark world beneath us, but we were here on the cliff, sheltered, keeping each other safe from loneliness. I leaned my head against Tom's shoulder, reluctant to speak.

Tom broke the silence. "I've wanted to say something to you but I don't know how."

Here it comes, I thought. He's going to tell me why he's hiding here. "Go ahead," I said. My fingernails cut into my palms.

He slid his arm around me and kissed my hair. "I've been trying to understand why I'm here," he said slowly.

I shut my eyes tight. "I don't know what you mean."

"Neither do I," he said, laughing a little. "I can't seem to leave here. I know I should try. I go down the road, but then . . . I forget. Something happens. I end up back by the pond again. I guess I'm waiting for you. I'm always waiting for you."

I looked up at him. "You wouldn't leave without telling me?" I asked, frightened.

"I'd find you and tell you first. I don't even know where I'm supposed to be going. I only know I should." He sighed. I felt the rise and fall of his chest under my hand.

"Tom," I whispered, "did you do something that you shouldn't have? Is that why you came here?"

"I don't know. I don't think so."

"Were you hurt? Do you think you were in some sort of accident and injured your head? Maybe you have amnesia. Sometimes people who have concussions can't remember what happened."

"I don't know that either."

"Where do you sleep?"

He didn't answer. I looked up at him again and he met my gaze. "You'll think I'm crazy," he whispered. "But I don't remember anymore. Sometimes I even wonder if I'm dead, but then you come and I know I can't be."

I hid my face. Oh, God, it can't be true. Drew is a liar.

"You're not a ghost," I said, trying hard to laugh. "Here's Troy. Who ever heard of a dog ghost? You just can't remember that you were in an accident and you ended up here."

Or, I thought, you did something awful and you don't want to remember what it was so you lost your memory and wandered off to this place.

"No matter what," I said suddenly, "we're both here now and that's all that counts. But we have to find another place for you to stay."

He leaned his face against my hair. "That's right. I remember now."

We sat quietly for a long time. Nothing else was important. Drew's nonsense wasn't worth a moment's consideration.

"Keller," Tom said, "I think that maybe Troy is dead

and he's trying to go away from here. I think he's staying because I can't say good-bye to him, and it's hurting him.''

I sat up and stared at him. "How can you say something like that? You can feel him! You're petting him right now!''

"But sometimes when I look at him, I almost understand whatever it is that I'm supposed to know.'' He looked away from me and down at his dog.

"What do you mean?'' I whispered.

"Sometimes,'' he said quietly, "I think I remember trying to get him out of the trap and not being able to pull him free. And then it seems to me that I can't get loose, either.'' He sighed. "I get so tired.''

"But you did get loose from the trap. Here you are.'' I pressed against him, turning my face toward his shirt. His white shirt. Just like his other white shirts. Or perhaps the same one.

"You feel this way because you were injured,'' I went on stubbornly. "That's why you're tired and why you can't remember anything.''

He looked away from me, out at the sky. "Maybe.''

I moved away and looked straight at him. "I'll show you how much you can remember. Let's try this. You lean back and relax, and I'll ask you questions. You say what comes to your mind.''

He grinned at me and my heart turned over. "Sure, Why not?'' He leaned back. "Go ahead.''

"What's your father's name?''

"That's easy. Donald Hurley,'' he said. "And my mother's name is Helen.''

"Tell me about the school you go to," I said.

"I go to Cascade High. I'm a senior and American Lit is my homeroom class."

"See?" I said. "Let's keep going. What's the teacher's name?"

"Mr. Callahan," he said promptly.

I was new at Cascade, but I hadn't heard of a Mr. Callahan. Of course, that didn't mean he wasn't there. "Do you know Miss Penny?" I asked.

He opened his eyes. "There's no Miss Penny at Cascade," he said. "I've been there so long that I know all the teachers."

"Then how about Miss Packer?" I asked quickly.

He shook his head. His grin faded a little. "No Packer. How about Miss Greely, the history teacher?"

I put my hands over my face. There was no Greely.

"What's wrong?"

I dropped my hands. "Nothing."

There was one question I could ask that would absolutely prove or disprove what Drew had told me, but I didn't want to ask it. I threw my arms around Tom's neck. "Let's not play this game anymore. I don't like it."

He pushed me away from him a little so that he could study my face. "What are you thinking about?"

I shook my head and tried to get closer to him again. "I'm not thinking anything."

"What is it?"

I closed my eyes and tears ran from under my eyelids. I could hardly form the words. "What's today's date?"

"I don't know exactly," he said slowly.

"What's the last date you remember?" I asked.

"September eleventh, I think," he said. "What are you getting at?"

"What year?" I whispered.

"Nineteen forty-six!" he said. "What's wrong? Why are you asking me these questions? What year is it supposed to be?"

I couldn't bring myself to tell him. I shook my head to clear it, to wake up from this nightmare.

He pulled me against his chest hard. "Tell me!" he said desperately. "What do you know?"

"Nothing." I sobbed. "I don't know anything."

Neither of us said a word for a long time. His tears fell on my hair. Once again in the forest below us I saw the misty houses and the streets with transparent, glimmering cars. Tears swam in my eyes and I blinked. The town was gone.

"What are we going to do?" I asked finally.

Tom held me tighter. "I don't know."

"Do you understand what's happened?"

"No. I'm afraid that if I let you go, you won't come back."

"I'll come back."

"Maybe you won't be able to," he said. "Or maybe if you come, I won't be able to be here."

"Don't say that!" I told him. "Don't even think about it. We're confused and somehow we've made a stupid mistake. We've been talking about impossible things."

I waited a long time before he answered. "I think you know that we're not confused," he said. The regret in his voice overwhelmed me.

"It'll seem different to us tomorrow," I cried wildly. "Wait and see! I'll come tomorrow and everything will make sense then." I remembered that my parents were coming Friday, but I didn't care. This was the only thing in my life that mattered.

"Oh, Keller," was all he said. He sounded exhausted.

"It's going to be all right," I said and I drew away from him. "I'm going home now. Get as much rest as you can and I'll be back tomorrow. Maybe I won't be able to get here right after school, but I'll make it, even if I have to come after dark—"

He put his fingers over my lips. "I won't be here. I'm never here when it gets dark."

"Then where are you?" I demanded. "I'll go wherever you are."

"You can't because I don't know myself."

I felt as if I were flying into a million jagged bits. "Don't say these things to me, Tom. Please. I beg you not to think that way. Whatever is wrong we'll fix! We'll make it turn out right!"

He pulled my arms from around his neck. "I'll walk you back to the pond," he said softly. "You're going to be sick if you stay here much longer."

"I never get sick when I'm with you," I protested. "Never."

"Come on." When we got to our feet, he almost seemed to stagger.

"Tom! Are you all right?"

He shook his head. "I don't know. Everything is so hard now. Sorry. I hate to have you see me like this."

"Stay here," I said. "I'll go and let you rest. You'll feel better tomorrow and we'll decide what to do then."

He smiled at me. "I'll see you next time."

I took a few steps, then looked back. He was stroking his dog again. And through them I could see the rock that they rested upon.

I looked away quickly, holding my breath, refusing to cry out. I would not look back again, I promised myself, because I was hallucinating. There was no telling what I'd imagine next.

After dinner, I swallowed one of the sedatives the doctor had given me and went to bed. In my sleep, I could hear the tags on Troy's collar jingle.

Fourteen

In class the next morning, while a voice on the PA system spluttered a message about the cafeteria menu, I poked Drew and said, "I need to ask you something."

He turned in his seat but he didn't smile. "What's up?"

I leaned close to him. He smelled nice, like starched cotton. "Do you have those photocopies with you?"

He raised his eyebrows. "No. They're home. Why?"

"I need to see them again."

"Why?"

I shut my eyes for a minutes, then said, "I didn't read the obituary."

"I read it. What do you want to know about it?"

I looked around to see if anyone was watching or listening. No one was, so I said, "Do you remember the first names of the boy's parents?"

He poked at his glasses. "No. Why?"

"Will you find out as soon as you get home and then call me?"

"Why?"

I was so tired and scared that my temper flared and I didn't stop to think. "Because I need to know! Can't you do one thing without having to know all the reasons?"

The people sitting nearest to us stared. Drew's face was unreadable. "I'll let you know," he said, and he turned to face the front of the room again.

I slid down in my seat, blinking hard to keep from crying. Before first period was over, I had to leave class to use my inhaler. The morning seemed months, years, long.

At lunchtime Jane stood in line behind me while I put a sandwich and a glass of water on my tray.

"I was thinking about you this morning," she said. "Max and I are going to a church mixer in North Grange tonight. You'd like it. Why don't you come with us? I bet Drew would come, too. We could go out for pizza afterward."

I pushed my tray forward, accidentally knocking it against the tray the boy ahead of me was sliding along with one hand. His milk carton tipped over and I gasped. "Sorry!" I cried.

"It's okay," he said. "It didn't spill." He looked at me curiously, then turned away.

I was making an idiot out of myself. My hands were shaking.

"What's wrong?" Jane asked. "Are you all right?"

"I'm fine," I lied. My heart was leaping frantically under my ribs. I'd used my inhaler too many times again.

"Well, how about tonight?" she asked. "Do you think you'd like to go with us?"

"My parents are coming from Seattle this afternoon," I told her, glad that I had an excuse. But I didn't want her to think that I was rude or that I didn't like her, so I added, "We're going to look at a house they're interested in buying. I don't know how long it'll take. Otherwise, I'd go with you. It sounds like fun."

"Maybe we can do it next month," she said.

"Sure." But I wouldn't go. I'd already risked all I could with Rose and Drew, and look what had happened with Drew.

I sat at the end of Drew's table and pretended to be interested in eating. Rose sat down next to me, with an open book in one hand. She hadn't finished her fourth-period homework and was trying to read an entire chapter during lunch. I was relieved that I wouldn't have to talk.

Drew moved next to me. "Let's walk around the school, lazybones," he said. "Come on."

He was so insistent that I got up from the table and let him take my hand.

"You look all stressed out," he said as we left the room.

I tried to force air out of my lungs, but had to stop walking before we ever reached the door leading outside. "I can't go," I said. "I can't breathe."

"Do you want me to take you home? I've got my car," he said.

131

I shook my head. "I've missed too much school already."

"Then come on out to the parking lot. We'll sit in the car for a few minutes and listen to the radio. You'll feel better." He squeezed my hand.

I looked at my watch. "The bell rings in ten minutes."

"Dr. Sennett prescribes ten minutes of music." Drew pulled me to the door. "I promise not to talk."

Once we were in the car, I began to relax. I tried to think about nothing at all. Drew didn't talk. He simply sat there, his head back, his eyes closed, listening to the music.

At last he touched my arm. "Time to go in, Keller."

I felt better, but I was still shaky. As we crossed the parking lot, he said, "We're going to sort everything out, you know. Don't worry any more."

I tried to take his advice, but I was anxious for the school day to end.

My parents were waiting at Grandmother's when I got home. "How are you feeling?" Mom asked, pushing my hair away from my face and studying me.

"Great," I said.

"You look thin," Dad said.

"She's been riding that bike nearly every day," Grandmother told them. "I don't think it's good for her."

"I don't like the cafeteria food at school so I skip lunch," I said hurriedly. "If we move close enough, I'll come home to eat every day. I'll be a fat pig by spring, you'll see. Now let's go see that house."

I succeeded in distracting them from my bike. They

put on their coats and we were ready to leave when the phone rang.

It's got to be Drew, I thought as I ran to answer it.

"Keller? I've got the obituary here," he said.

"Okay. Tell me the names." I pressed the phone against my ear so hard that it hurt.

"The father was Donald and the mother was Helen."

My legs shook. I swallowed hard. "Thanks," I said.

"You asked that guy what his parents' names were, didn't you?" Drew asked. "They're the same, aren't they?"

"I've got to go now. My family's waiting for me."

"Keller, please don't go out to the pond again."

I hung up. My fingers were stiff and didn't want to let go of the phone.

"Keller?" Grandmother asked. "Was that Drew?"

I nodded.

She turned to my parents. "He's the grandson of a friend of mine. He's such a nice boy, and he's been taking Keller out. You'll like him."

I followed them out to the porch and looked in the direction of Deerfield Pond. Sun shone there, through slanting, slate-colored clouds. Tom was dead, truly dead. The boy who saved me from drowning didn't exist. I had imagined everything.

No. I'd nearly drowned — I didn't imagine that — and Tom had rescued me. I knew him. I'd walked in the woods with him and talked to him. He'd kissed me. He was more real to me than anyone else.

How could this be explained? There had been a terrible mistake made somewhere. Oh, Tom, what had really happened all those long years ago when you dived under the water to help your dog? If you really died then, are you dreaming now, and have I been caught up in your dream? Or am I the one who dreams? Have I been sick and lonely for so long that I'd invent someone to love?

What am I going to do now?

Following Grandmother's directions, Dad drove us to the house Mrs. Ashburn had shown Grandmother and me. He stopped in front for a moment, so that we could look at it.

"It's certainly big enough," Mom said.

"It needs paint," Dad said.

"There are five acres of land in back," Grandmother said. "And a creek."

Dad pulled in the driveway behind a pickup truck. We walked up the steps to the front door and Dad rang the bell. Inside, we could hear footsteps approaching.

A tall man with oily, graying hair opened the door. He smiled, his rubbery lips pulled back to show yellow teeth.

"You the Parrishes?" he asked. He stuck out his hand. His fingernails were rimmed with black.

Ugh, I thought. On sight, I hated him and his house, but my dad shook hands with him politely and we walked inside.

The living room was large, with many windows and a fireplace that took up most of the end wall. It probably had been beautiful once, but now it was shabby and terribly dirty. Mom and I exchanged glances.

"It needs a good cleaning," Grandmother said, openly disgusted.

The tall man frowned at her and turned to my father. "I've been living here by myself since my sister died," he said. "It's too big for me, so I'm moving to North Grange, to an apartment."

"I see," Dad said uncomfortably. "I suppose we should look around the rest of the house, Mr. . . . ah, Elwood?"

"Elwood Bruce," the man said eagerly. "But you go ahead and call me Elwood."

A stone sat on my chest. I couldn't speak. My ears rang. Elwood Bruce had been the one who set the traps at Deerfield Pond.

My parents were moving off with the man, into the dining room where a dusty chandelier hung over a battered table.

"Keller?" Grandmother said. "Are you coming?"

Elwood Bruce stared at me because I was staring at him. Blood pounded at my temples.

"What's wrong with her?" he asked Grandmother.

My parents turned back, alarmed.

"Keller?" Mom asked.

My eyes burned. My fingernails dug into my palms. "You," I said. "You did it."

"What the hell's wrong with the kid?" Elwood Bruce demanded.

"You killed him!" I shouted. "You're the one who set the traps at Deerfield Pond. You killed Tom."

The color faded from Elwood Bruce's face. "What are you talking about?"

"He told me what you did!" I cried, and I raised my fists and ran toward him.

135

"Keller!" my dad shouted, grabbing me. "What's going on?"

"Get her out of here!" Elwood Bruce yelled. "Get that crazy little freak out of my house. Get her out!"

I couldn't stop shouting. Dad shook me, then threw his arms around me. "My God, Keller, what's wrong? What are you talking about?"

A great fist closed inside my chest, squeezing out the last of my breath. I opened my mouth, struggling for air. My vision filled with flickering light. There was no air here. No air in all the world. I clutched my father's jacket.

"The hospital!" I heard Grandmother cry.

No air no air no air no air. Fear slid over me like thick mud. Then after that came the dark.

I thought only that this was what it had been like for Tom when he drowned.

Fifteen

After three days, I was moved from the hospital critical care section to an ordinary room. I still slept most of the time, and I still needed oxygen, but sometimes I was awake enough to understand where I was. I was too tired to care, however.

On Tuesday afternoon, Rose and Jane came to see me. "We wanted to bring flowers," Rose said, "but we called your mother first, thank goodness, and she said we'd better not bring real ones." She handed me a bouquet of beautiful silk flowers. "We're glad you're better."

Jane handed me a small, flat package wrapped in pink paper. "Open it."

I pulled off the paper. Inside I found a book of cartoons. "Thanks," I told her. "I need something to make me laugh."

"You need Drew, then," Rose said. "He can mak anybody laugh."

I didn't respond. Drew hadn't been to see me, bu Grandmother had told me that he called twice a day. wasn't ready to see him. Maybe I never would be. I' feel like an idiot.

How much did everybody know about what happene at Elwood Bruce's house? Dad had asked me the morn ing I was taken out of critical care to explain what I' been talking about the afternoon I got sick. I'd pre tended that I couldn't remember. I'd been afraid to as him if he and Mom had decided to buy that house. Whe he'd finally mentioned it, he told me that they weren' considering it. They were looking at a better place.

"But," he'd told me, "we'd like to know what wa going on at the Bruce house. When you're better, we' talk about it."

Grandmother had said that they'd asked Drew if h knew Elwood Bruce and Drew told them that all th kids in school hated the man because he was so mean But sooner or later I'd have to account for what hap pened.

Looking at Rose and Jane, I wondered if they'd hear anything about the scene in the old house. I couldn't tel by their expressions. They didn't stay long but promise to come back again.

I dozed for a while after they left and woke up wit a start to find Drew standing at the window, lookin out.

"I hate it when someone's in the room with me whe I'm sleeping," I said.

He turned. "Gee, it's nice that you're so glad to see me. You must be feeling better because you're about as cheerful as a crocodile." He sat down next to the bed. "How much longer will you have that tube in your nose? I was thinking about kissing you, but I wasn't sure if something would explode."

I touched the oxygen tube and sighed. "I bet I look like something from a horror movie."

"That's close. Hey, I come bearing strange and wonderful gifts. Look at this." He dug through his pockets and came up with a small, shiny object. He put it on the tray in front of me.

"What's that? It looks like a robot."

"I don't know what it is. It showed up at the back door last night and bellowed until I let it in." He gave it a push and the stiff little figure whirred loudly and waddled toward me.

I laughed weakly. "That's ridiculous."

He dug through his pockets again. "Okay, if that doesn't impress you, how about this?" He pulled out a small plastic duck and squeezed it. It produced an incredibly loud honk. "For your bath."

"Thank you, but I take showers."

He reached into his jacket pocket and took out a square package. "Try this, oh spoiled brat."

I unwrapped the gift, unable to suppress a smile. He'd given me a glass ball paperweight, one with a scene inside. I shook it. Instead of snow, the ball filled with tiny, bright autumn leaves that settled gradually over a house that looked like the old place at Deerfield Pond.

I had to clear my throat. "It's beautiful," I said.

He grinned, pleased. I saw that he wasn't wearing braces anymore.

"No more tin grin," I said shakily.

"My orthodontist actually runs that junkyard outside of town," he said. "I was supposed to be wearing braces for another year, but Dad got behind in the payments so Turk dropped by and yanked out my wires."

"Stop," I said, holding up my hand. "I'm too sick to start laughing at you."

He took my hand. "You look wonderful. Your cheeks are pink and your eyes shine. I like you an awful lot." He leaned over and kissed my forehead.

Then he straightened up and took something else out of his pocket. He held it out to me. "Here's something that will get you out of bed faster than a miracle cure. Have a look."

It was a newspaper clipping.

"Is it something about Tom?" I asked quietly. Tom. He haunted my drugged sleep, his smile so clear sometimes that I could have sworn I was at the farm with him. Awake, I didn't dare think about him. Asleep, I couldn't stop.

"Read the clipping," Drew said. He leaned back in his chair to wait.

I unfolded the article. It was from the North Grange paper, dated the day before.

"Death on the Highway. Elwood Bruce, retired, died last night when his truck overturned on the highway two miles north of Cascade. C. Benson Kirk, a witness, told the county police that Bruce apparently lost control of

he truck when he swerved to avoid hitting a large dog
hat ran out on the road.''

There was more, but I folded the article and handed
t back to Drew. I was glad Bruce was dead — and
shamed of feeling that way. "Did you tell anyone?" I
asked.

"That this was the guy who set the traps at the pond
a long time ago? No. Your family asked me if I knew
what you were so upset about when you met him. They
said you were talking about Bruce killing someone.''

"What did you tell them?"

Drew shrugged. "That he had a bad reputation around
own for being a drunk. And he did, too. As a matter of
act, Julie Casper lives across the street from him, and
she said he'd been dead drunk for the last four days. I
old your family that you'd probably heard some of the
rumors about him.''

"Did they believe you?"

Drew grinned. "Why not? If you don't tell them any
different, they'll forget all about it sooner or later.''

I shook the glass ball and watched the leaves fall again.
"Why are you helping me?" I asked finally.

He didn't say anything for a minute. When he spoke
again, his voice was rough. "I don't understand what's
been going on out at the pond, but if your family and
everybody else get mixed up in it, I have a hunch that
you'll be worse off than you are now.''

"I know."

"You shouldn't go out there anymore. If he's really
there, Tom's ghost, I mean, then you're only making it

harder on yourself by running back all the time. It's not as if anything real could happen."

I turned my head away. Tom had kissed me. That was real.

"Sooner or later people are going to wonder what you're doing there. You won't be able to explain it. You know what everybody would think if they knew."

"That I'm crazy. Why don't you think that?"

He sighed. "I guess I believe you because you drew the picture of him before you saw his photograph in the old newspaper clipping." He took the ball from me and shook it. The leaves drifted. "What are you going to do, Keller?"

My eyes filled with tears. "I don't know. He must be wondering where I am. He waits for me, and when I don't come, he worries."

Drew seemed to be concentrating on the leaves in the ball. "Maybe he knows where you are."

"What do you mean?"

Drew looked at me. "I went out there. I didn't see him, but I walked over to the pond and called out to him. I told him where you are and that you couldn't come for a while. Not that I didn't think I was acting crazy."

I swallowed hard, blinking away tears. "Thanks," I said. "Maybe he heard you."

Drew shrugged. "It was funny, though. I thought I heard a sort of jingling sound, like a little bell."

I shut my eyes and tears leaked across my temples. "The metal tags on Troy's collar."

Drew put the paperweight down and rubbed his arms. "I'm getting goose bumps."

I reached out my hand to him and he took it. "I appreciate what you did."

"So what comes next?" he asked.

"I don't know," I said. I was tired. I didn't have answers to anything or know what could happen next. "I can't stay away. I can't leave him there alone. I'd be dead if it hadn't been for him. And he is . . . ." I couldn't talk any longer.

"Don't you see that this can't go anywhere?" Drew asked.

I turned my face away from him and pulled my hand loose from his.

"I mean, he's dead and you're alive," Drew said. "Nothing can happen. You can't stay with him and he can't stay with you."

"You don't know that," I whispered.

"Oh, jeez," Drew said softly. "Please don't go back. Please don't do something stupid."

"He's . . . everything!" I whispered. "With him, I'm always well. We're alike somehow. If it hadn't been for him, I'd be dead."

Drew pulled off his glasses and rubbed his eyes, hard. "I can't fight that," he said. He got up and shoved his glasses back on. "I'd better split. Look, if you need anything, call me. If there's ever anything I can do, tell me. Sooner or later — "

"No," I said. "Don't say it."

He hesitated, then bent and kissed me again, that time

on my lips. "That's the first time I ever kissed anybody with a tube up her nose," he said. "I'd probably like it better without the tube. See you later, Keller." And he was gone.

I shook the paperweight again and put it down. The little silver robot began whirring and walked off the edge of the tray.

Drew had left the newspaper article behind. I crumpled it into a ball and dropped it into the wastebasket next to my bed.

I wondered if I knew the dog who'd been on that dark road.

Sixteen

I was released from the hospital on the following Friday afternoon. As we drove on Birch Road, leaves blew in tumbling streams ahead of a cold wind. I wanted Dad to drive past Grandmother's house straight to the pond, but I didn't dare ask.

Tom was on my mind. He wasn't an idle thought that entertained me in pensive moments. He was all there was. But even though I thought about him constantly, my vision of him was fading. It was as if the more I reached for him, the farther away he drew, until I was no longer certain how he looked.

Had he heard Drew when Drew went to the pond to tell him where I was? Or was it impossible for Drew to communicate with him? Did he think I had abandoned him? I had to go to the pond. But once we got to Grandmother's house, my parents shepherded me upstairs and put me to bed as if I were a small child.

"Thank God you're all right," Mom said. She patted the quilt that she'd laid over me, as if it, too, needed comforting. "If we'd known how you were going to react to that dreadful man, we'd never have taken you to see his house."

Dad came in then and leaned against the door. "According to Drew Sennett, there was a lot of animosity in town between the high school kids and Bruce."

I avoided my father's gaze and looked out the window. The birches bent and shed leaves into the wind. They blew toward the pond. Toward Tom.

"She's too tired to talk about it," Mom said to Dad. There was a warning in her voice.

Dad shrugged. "Sorry, Keller. I guess I still feel uneasy about the situation. We don't understand what happened."

"Jack," Mom said flatly.

Dad came to the bed, bent over me and kissed me on the forehead. "Sorry, baby. Sorry." He fussed with the quilt for a moment, kissed me again, and left the room.

Mom settled back in the chair next to the bed. "He was frantic. You'll have to forgive him. I've never seen him like that. I thought he was going back to that house and kill that repulsive man — and he didn't even know what was wrong, just that something about the man upset you." Mom followed my gaze. "Fall's here," she said, sighing. Then she looked back at me. "Maybe someday you can tell us what was wrong."

I shut my eyes to close her out. "I'd been feeling bad all day," I said, reciting the speech I'd rehearsed for this moment. "And everybody had been telling me sto-

146

ries about Elwood Bruce. I can't really remember what happened. I guess I went to pieces. Stupid. You know how people get when they're sick. And I had cramps on top of everything else. I'm so embarrassed I could die.''

Mom took my hand and squeezed it. ''Don't let yourself get upset now,'' she said. ''It's all over.''

''And you won't buy that house,'' I said, needing reassurance.

''Oh, no,'' she said quickly. ''We couldn't even if we wanted to. The man died a few days ago in an accident. I'm sure the house will be tied up with legal matters for a long time. We've just about decided on a house a few blocks away from your friend.''

''Rose?'' I asked, surprised.

''No, Drew.'' She grinned at me. ''He's nice. He has a strange sense of humor, though. I'm never sure if I should laugh.''

''Laugh,'' I told her. I shut my eyes again. ''You'll disappoint him if you don't laugh, no matter what he says.''

''Is he your new boyfriend?'' Mom asked hesitantly, after a small silence.

My heart lurched. Tom. ''When did I ever have an *old* boyfriend?'' I asked her. ''Drew's just a friend, that's all.''

''Ah.'' Mom got up, patted my quilt again, and walked to the door. ''Well, you sleep now, until dinner. And in a few days we'll take you to see the other house.''

She closed the door behind her and my eyes snapped open.

Tom.

I got up and went to the window. The wind had torn open the cloudy sky and the afternoon sun shone in my eyes, dazzling me.

Tomorrow I'll be stronger, I told myself. I'll get out somehow and look for Tom. And we'll make plans.

On Saturday morning, Mom and Grandmother went grocery shopping, leaving me with Dad. Half an hour later, Mom called. Grandmother's car had stalled in North Grange. Dad took off in his car after questioning me about whether or not I felt well enough to be left alone for a while.

"Go rescue them," I said. "There are some great stores in North Grange, and if you leave them there very long, they'll spend all your money."

He laughed. The moment his car disappeared down the block, I grabbed my jacket and headed for the garage to get my bike.

The morning fog hadn't burned off yet, so I rode between golden trees standing in misty silence. My legs were weak and they trembled, but I wouldn't consider turning back. I must find Tom, see him, touch his face. What would happen after that was beyond my imaginings.

I left my bike in the driveway and walked toward the pond, barely visible in the mist. The tall, yellow grass was beaded with crystal drops of moisture and whispered against the legs of my jeans. Jeweled spider webs stretched across my path, and I, afraid to disturb any fragile structure in that veiled morning, stepped aside and passed cautiously.

The trees around the pond dripped softly. I heard a

fish splash in the water. "Tom," I said, "are you here?"

The mist over the pond hung still. I thought I heard something move in the woods.

The mist on the far side of the pond stirred like a curtain in a light wind. Through it stepped a deer. I watched it while it drank at the pond.

My pulse beat in my throat and my eyes filled with tears. The deer was beautiful, and I was not quite sane. "Have you seen Tom?" I asked.

The deer raised its head and looked at me for a long moment, then turned and walked slowly back into the woods. The mist closed behind it.

I found a log, sat down, and curled my arms around my knees. I would not be able to find my way through the woods in the fog, and so I couldn't go searching for Tom. I'd have to wait.

After a while the fog thinned and lifted. In the woods, moisture dripped like rain. I walked toward the cliff, searching under the trees for Tom and his dog. Sometimes I stopped and spoke their names. My quiet voice raised echoes.

I stepped out on the rock that overlooked the wooded valley. The sun shone here, hard and brassy, and I looked down at the houses and streets of North Grange.

Hadn't I always known they were there? Wasn't the unbroken forest only a memory of Tom's that I'd shared? Or had he been dreaming dreams of another time that I, awake, had somehow been able to share?

Or was I the dreamer?

I covered my face with my hands. I couldn't answer my own questions.

Now, suddenly, I was afraid. I turned back toward the woods and shouted for Tom, screamed for him. Birds flew shrieking from the trees. Ahead of me an unseen animal raced on the path, then crashed to the left and fled. At the pond I called Tom's name, begging him to answer me. Only the frightened birds responded.

I ran across the field toward the house and pounded on the front door until my hands ached. "You have to answer me, Tom," I wept. "Please, oh, please."

No answer. I leaped from the front porch and ran to the back, throwing myself against the door. It swung open and I rushed inside. "Tom!"

The rooms were empty, except for dust and shadows. I ran from one to another, stumbling on warped floors. No one had been there for years. There were no bright curtains in the kitchen, no mother to make lemonade for a son on a hot day, no trace of a family.

I stood on the back porch for a moment before plunging back across the field. He had to be there, somewhere. I couldn't have waited those long days in the hospital for heartbreak such as this, I told myself. By the force of my will, I would call him back from wherever he had drifted.

"Tom!" I cried when I reached the pond. "Come to the pond! I have to see you one more time. Oh, please, one more time!"

I saw the dog first, walking slowly out of the woods, looking around as if bewildered by the bright light.

"Come, Troy!" I called. "Come here."

The dog stopped and stared at me. His tail wagged

hesitantly, but instead of running to me, he sat suddenly.

I realized he was too weak to walk, and I hurried to him, ashamed that I had called him from his rest. I knelt and stroked him. Under my hands, he lay down and abruptly slept. He was barely breathing. I bent and hugged him. My tears dripped on him.

But where was Tom? When I looked up, I expected him to step out of the woods, smiling. But he wasn't there.

I got to my feet and started into the woods again.

"Tom?" I called.

He was standing off to one side of the path, far back under the trees.

"Keller," he said. His voice was faint and weary.

I left the path and ran toward him, but he vanished into the shadows. I called his name but he didn't return.

Behind me, Troy whimpered. I turned back to go to the dog.

Tom was there on the path, between me and Troy. I hesitated, surprised. The distance between us increased, and I broke into a run, afraid that I would lose him even as I found him.

"Tom, wait!"

Then he was standing by the dog, puzzled, as if he had no control over where he went. I wasn't certain that he saw me.

"Tom, it's me, Keller. Please wait."

Then, suddenly, I knew he saw me again. He smiled and reached out his hand.

"It's you," he said. "Sometimes I thought you were here, but I was never sure. And sometimes I couldn't get here, and I was afraid you'd be looking for me and give up."

"Never," I told him as I took his hand. "I'd never give up."

"Your friend told me you couldn't come," he said.

"He didn't see you. He didn't know if you heard him, but I'm glad you did. I dreamed of being here so many times. It seemed real."

"You were very sick."

"Yes," I said. "But I'm all right now. Tell me about you. How have you been? Have you made plans for yourself yet?"

He shook his head and looked away from me. "There aren't any plans that I can make. I just seem to wait."

"We'll find a way. There's always a way to make plans." I spoke rapidly, my mouth dry. "We've just confused ourselves — "

"No," he said. "We know."

"I can't lose you now." I was suddenly terrified, and I grabbed his arm.

"Oh, Keller," he said, and his voice broke.

But I knew then that I was losing him. I felt a chill, as if I touched a shadow. He stepped back, his face pale, and he pulled free of me.

"I don't think I can stay, no matter how hard I try," he said. "I get so tired, I'm so cold."

"Tom!" I reached for him, but he was already beyond my touch. I saw him with Troy at the edge of the woods, and as I turned toward him, he faded, faded, until I could see only the shape of him glimmering against the backdrop of the deep woods.

I ran toward where he had been and turned in circles, searching, crying. "Don't leave me here. We'll find a way. Oh, Tom, don't do this."

My tears were scalding. "What will I do without you?" I cried. "Tell me what to do."

He didn't answer. I tripped clumsily and fell to my knees, shouting his name over and over.

"Oh, Keller, stop," I heard.

Drew knelt beside me and grabbed my hands. I leaned against him and he put his arms around me.

"Tom's gone away," I said. "What am I going to do?"

"Come on. Stand up." He urged me softly, pulling me up. "Let me take you home. You can't stay here."

"I can't leave," I cried and I jerked away from him, starting into the woods. "I have to get him back!" I shouted savagely. "He can't leave me. Tom! You can't leave!"

I was wild with grief and rage. Every time Drew reached for me, I slapped at his hands. He followed me as I ran to the cliff, and when I returned to the pond, weeping, he still followed.

"Tom, come back!" I shouted. "If you don't come back, I'll find a way to follow you. Tom!"

There he was again. Drew saw him, I know, because I heard him suck in his breath. Tom was poised at the edge of the pond, as if he was about to jump in. The water stirred near the place where the old beaver dam had been replaced long before with stones.

I realized suddenly what Tom was going to do. "Don't go in the water!" I screamed. "It's too late."

But Tom was gone, under water again searching for his dog, and both of them were captive in some awful echo of the tragedy.

The scene replayed itself again and again. Tom standing by the pond, Tom under water, Tom standing by the pond again.

"Keller, stop it!" Drew shouted. He grabbed and held me. "Stop calling him! Let him go!"

I wrenched myself free and ran to the pond, but Drew was right behind me, and he grabbed me again. "For God's sake, Keller, let him alone! Can't you see what you're doing?"

I turned blindly to him. "What do you want? Get away from me!"

"Let him go," Drew said. "You're making it terrible for him. Just let him go."

My vision was blurred by hot tears, but I saw Tom once again go into the pond, and I threw myself after him, floundering in the water, reaching for him until it was over my head.

Drew dragged me back and wrapped his arms around me. "If you don't leave him alone, I'll force you home and tell your parents," he said. "Keller, they'll lock you up. Listen to me! It's time to let him go."

I collapsed against him, finally understanding. It was over. The pond water lay flat and quiet.

After a long moment, Drew said, "I'm going to take you to my house. No one's home there. I'll run your clothes through the dryer. We'll tell your family that I took you out for a ride and kept you longer than I should have.''

I didn't care. I couldn't imagine caring about anything again. Drew led me to his car.

"I went by to see you and no one was home," Drew said. "I looked in the garage and your bike was gone, so I figured you might be here. Listen, when we pass your grandmother's house, duck your head if they're there. Okay?''

The driveway was empty. "Just let me off here," I said dully.

"Not a chance," Drew said quietly. "I can't trust you until you're too far away to run back to the pond."

I leaned my head back, defeated. "I'm ruining your upholstery."

"You also ruined my new jacket," he said. "That'll teach me to buy dry-clean-only clothes when I'm involved with you. You're strictly wash-and-wear, Keller."

At his house, he took me in the back door and got me a bathrobe to wear while my clothes went through a dryer cycle. He changed his own clothes and made me a cup of tea in the kitchen.

"Are you feeling all right?" he asked when he gave me the cup.

I nodded. "I'm never sick when I'm with Tom," I said.

"Jeez," he said. "That's just dandy. So it's okay to practically drown yourself when you're at the pond, is that it?''

I looked down into my cup.

He pushed his glasses up on his head and rubbed his

eyes. "What I can't understand is why I'm crazy about you, Keller. I think you're nuts. I just watched you nearly kill yourself over another guy, and here I am, ready to lie for you and prepared to be turned into cat food by your parents."

"I'm grateful," I whispered. "Don't think I'm not."

"Ha," he said reflectively. "I'm not sure your gratitude is going to be worth it."

I began crying again. "I'm sorry. What else can I say?"

"Nothing." He leaned back in his chair.

I wiped my eyes. "You saw him, didn't you?"

He nodded.

"What am I going to do?"

He looked at me with more compassion than anger. "I don't know. Didn't you ever think that maybe everything that was supposed to happen has already happened?"

"What do you mean?" His words chilled me. I folded my arms over my chest.

Drew settled his glasses on his nose. "Tom and the pond seem to be linked together. Maybe he's been waiting all these years as a sort of guardian of the pond, in case someone else got into trouble there."

I stared at him, devastated at the thought that Tom might be condemned to an existence like that, waiting until the end of time for disasters at the pond.

"Or maybe," he went on, not looking at me, "he waited because he knew that you, Keller Parrish, would need rescuing some day. And he stayed on with you when he wasn't supposed to, but now he has to leave."

I looked down at my tea again.

Drew sighed. "That's it, I'll bet. I guess I knew that much."

"Do you think I'll see him again?" I whispered.

"Ah, Keller," Drew exclaimed, his voice cracking. "Give me a break, will you?"

I reached one hand across the table and took his.

"Just don't do anything stupid, okay?" he said. His look was significant. I dropped my gaze. He was afraid that I'd kill myself.

"Okay, Keller?" he yelled. "Promise me you won't try. It won't do any good, you know."

"Nothing will do any good," I said. My sadness was so profound that I could barely make myself heard.

"That's not true," Drew said. "I'll do you good. If you give me a chance, I'll make you laugh. And sometimes I'll even kiss you if you promise not to hit me too hard."

My laughter was mixed with tears. He was right. He truly did me good. But I couldn't imagine ever being free from my grief.

The buzzer on the dryer signaled that my clothes were dry, so I got dressed and Drew took me home. My parents and Grandmother were waiting, furious.

Drew, holding my hand, apologized. "I haven't had her alone for days," he said hastily. "So we went for a ride." He blinked behind his glasses and smiled ingratiatingly at Grandmother. "Don't tell Granny, Mrs. P. She'll put Gimpy Callahan and the Monday Evening Mud

Wrestling Club on my track, and I'm as good as dead by dinnertime.''

There was a moment of awful silence, and then my father burst out laughing. Drew had maneuvered me past the crisis.

I left them together and went upstairs to rest. Tom drifted hazily through my exhausted dreams, and I didn't wake until late in the evening.

Pale moonlight illuminated Birch Road. From my window I watched the night and slow tears dripped on my hands.

''Keller,'' Tom whispered from the dark, ''see you next time.''

Seventeen

The next morning, my parents went to church with Grandmother, leaving me sitting in the sunny kitchen with a plate of apple turnovers and the Sunday newspaper. As soon as they went out of sight, I dressed quickly. I had an errand to run before they got back. I'd left my bike at the pond, and so far my family hadn't missed it. But I couldn't count on their forgetting about it.

Someone knocked lightly on the back door. I considered not answering, but when I peeked out the kitchen window to see who'd come, I reconsidered and opened the door.

Drew stood on the porch, grinning down at me. "You're dressed already!" he said. "I was hoping to catch you in your jammies. I figured they'd be the kind that had feet on them, and maybe a bunny sewn on the pocket."

"Why aren't you in church?" I demanded as I let him

in. "I thought you were a Sunday school teacher, not a weirdo who creeps around spying on women in their pajamas."

"I talked Granny into taking my class." He helped himself to a turnover and sat down.

"What are you doing here?" I asked. "Not that I'm not glad to see you. But what's the occasion?"

"We'd better get your wheels," he said. He pulled the comics section across the table and opened it. "Or did you forget them?"

"Of course not. I was just leaving."

"I'll give you a ride on my bike," he said, looking up. "That's faster than walking."

He was right. "Let's get started then," I said. "I don't want them to come back and find me gone. I'm in enough trouble as it is."

He crammed the last of the turnover in his mouth and opened the door for me. "The carriage awaits, madam," he said.

We rode over a long carpet of leaves, and a bright blue sky above us was almost too bright to bear. Neither of us spoke.

This would be the last of it, I thought. Bringing home my abandoned bike would be the end of the story of Tom and me. No one else but Drew knew that he'd ever been at Deerfield Pond. After a while Drew would probably forget that he'd seen Tom. He'd convince himself that I'd imagined the whole thing. He might even come to believe that I was more than a little bit crazy.

The frightening thing was that maybe I would come to believe that, too. It seemed impossible that I could ever betray Tom by denying that I'd known him, but might it not happen after weeks and months and years went by and I was still alone? I wasn't going to turn a corner somewhere and see him coming toward me. He was gone. He'd returned to the place he'd come from that day to keep his appointment with me.

Drew let me off his bike in the driveway of Deerfield Pond. My bike was where I left it, and it was wet with dew that sparkled in the cold, bright light. I set it upright, then put it down again. I wasn't ready to leave yet.

"You don't have to wait for me," I said to Drew.

"What are you going to do?"

I couldn't look at him. "I want to walk around for a while."

"I'll go with you."

I shook my head. "Please let me go by myself."

"No." He put down his bike. "You want to walk over to the pond? See the house? What?"

"See the pond. Maybe walk around a little."

"You won't have much time, not if you want to get back before the thundering herd rides up after church."

"I know." I started out into the field, not looking back to see if Drew was following me.

A pheasant rose from the grass at my feet, crying out in alarm. Behind me, Drew laughed, said "Jeez," and laughed again.

In the pond, the goldfish hung suspended in the water, close to the surface where the sun warmed them. Yellow leaves stirred on the ripples.

"I wish I could have seen the first dam that was here,"

Drew said. "The one the beavers built. But that was a long time ago."

A long time ago.

I walked around the pond, remembering where the deer had come down to drink. Of course, there'd been no deer here for more years than I'd been alive, I told myself. Somehow I'd been enchanted by Tom's vivid memory, his love of animals and of this place. If I saw hoof prints even now in the soft earth at the edge of the pond, it was because some of the magic was still with me.

"Last night I thought I heard Tom talk to me," I said. I looked at the water, not Drew. I didn't want to see the expression of disbelief I was afraid he wore.

"What did he say?" Drew asked. There was quiet resignation in his voice.

"He said, 'Keller, see you next time.' "

Drew was silent for a moment, then said, "Is he here now?"

"I don't think so."

"Then what did he mean?"

I shrugged and bit my lip. "I don't know. I don't think I'm ever going to find him here again. You know the feeling you get when something's sure to happen? The hunch that lets you take it for granted? Well, I don't have that. I'm just . . . blank. Hollow. I don't have anything to look forward to."

Drew kicked a pebble into the pond. "That's a rotten way to look at life."

I shrugged again. "I never did have anything to look

forward to except more of what I was so tired of already. Trying to keep from being sick but being sick anyway. Only having friends for a little while because I'm boring and embarrassing and there are a lot of things I can't do.''

"You think it's worse than it is. And you aren't exactly easy to get to know.''

"You managed.''

He laughed. "Only because I've got a thick skin and not much pride,'' he said. "And you're not sick all the time, Keller. When you are, most people probably feel sorry for you — ''

"I don't want anyone feeling sorry for me!'' I cried. "Tom didn't feel sorry for me, so I looked forward to coming here and seeing him. He made me well. I was safe with him. He told me honest things about how he felt. He could even say that he was lonely. That's something I never wanted to admit about myself, not to anybody.''

"Yeah.'' Drew shoved his hands in his pockets and looked across the pond toward the line of poplars. The tops of the trees stirred in a thin, high gust of wind. A scattering of small gold leaves tore loose and fluttered down. "Well, standing here listening to you, I feel lonely for the first time in my life.''

I was surprised at the bitterness in his voice. "I'm sorry,'' I said.

He shook his head impatiently. "Oh, the hell with it. Look, let's be practical. If you felt safe with him, you can feel safe again. With me, for instance. Or pick someone else. Try expecting fun instead of a hard time. Or if you can't do that, at least try to take things as they come, good and bad. Roll with 'em.''

He sounded like all the people I'd ever known who didn't have any idea what I went through but still felt qualified to give me advice. I glared at him. ''I hate it when people tell me how much better they could live my life for me. Stop it!''

He kicked another pebble. ''You can be a royal pain in the ass sometimes, Keller. You know that?''

''Then go home!'' I retaliated. ''Go on. Get out of here and let me alone.''

''And leave you to think up some stunt? Forget it.''

I raised my chin defiantly. ''I'm not going to drown myself, if that's what you think. Go away, Drew. I don't want to talk to you anymore.''

I let him stare into my eyes until he was satisfied. ''Jeez,'' he said. ''Okay.'' He straightened his shoulders. ''Remember that you don't have a lot of time before you should go home.''

I watched him walk away. Once he stopped and looked down, then bent to pick up something. He glanced at me, put whatever it was in his pocket, and ducked through the trees surrounding the pond. When he was out of sight, I looked across the water.

''Tom,'' I said softly, ''if I was wrong and you're still here, please say something.''

Waiting, I heard only the wind hissing in the tops of the poplars. A school of goldfish in the pond streamed slowly in wide circles, following some pattern known only to them. They disappeared in glittering spangles of sunlight and reappeared farther away, then sank out of sight. The wind grew stronger, colder.

When there was no more time, I left, following Drew's path through the trees and across the field. I didn't look up until I reached the driveway.

Drew waited there, watching me approach, hands in his pockets. "We have to hurry now," he said.

I picked up my bike. "Thanks for waiting. I'm sorry about the things I said."

"No problem." He held out his closed fist. "Here. I found something you might want to have."

"What is it?" I stretched out my hand.

Drew dropped a small metal tag in my palm. It was stamped with a number and a date, 1946. I closed my fingers over it.

"Troy's dog tag," I said. "Thank you." My eyes blurred with tears. I looked at the tag again and rubbed my thumb over the date. In 1946, there were deer here at the pond, and beavers, too. And Tom, who would wait for me until I came and then stay too long.

I swallowed hard, "Let's go," I said.

Without a word, Drew rode down the driveway.

I looked across the field. Oh please, I thought, let him hear me once more. "Tom," I said aloud, "I'll see you next time."

Then I shoved the dog tag in my pocket and took off after Drew. When I reached the road, he was far ahead. I pedaled harder.

"Drew! Wait for me!" I shouted.

He looked back over his shoulder, then suddenly laughed. "Catch me if you can!"

I took a deep, free breath and bent over my handle-bars. "Look out!" I called him. "Here I come!"